Olly gaped open-mouthed at the new locum GP.

This is not what I expected.

She was petite—elfin, almost—with a graceful, slim but womanly figure which he couldn't help but notice due to her clothing. Or what there was of it. Her dark, almost black hair was cut short at the back, but at the front it was long and multi-coloured—cyan-blue, purple and pink streaks fell across her face. Her arms were layered with bangles and she had a red jewel in her belly button. She twirled and swirled and sashayed as she led the class in 'undulation one'.

'All right, Olly?' his dad asked, staring at his son in amusement.

How can this woman be a GP? She doesn't look like one.

But what was a GP *supposed* to look like? There was a shimmery wrap around her waist, tightly sheathing her perfectly curved bottom, and it tinkled and glimmered as she moved. Then, as she pointed her tiny feet, he noticed tattoos and nail polish and toe-rings, before his eyes rose back up to her face to see large brown eyes, rosy cheeks and a cheeky smile.

Patrick lea_____ _____ _____ to whisper in h__ _____ ___ __ ___ a hung___

Olly____

Dear Reader,

I have to admit to you that there are three pet rats in my house. Yes—three. Blaze, Finlay and Harper are three brothers that I rescued, and one day, whilst they were out of their cage, playing on my shoulder, I wondered if there had ever been a Mills & Boon® heroine with pet rats who also needed rescuing herself?

That single question inspired this story! My heroine, Lula, came instantly—in all her glory—and Olly, my hero, quickly followed. I knew that these two, together, would create a love story that we all could fall in love with.

I absolutely adore their story and hope you do too.

Love

Louisa xx

HIS PERFECT BRIDE?

BY
LOUISA HEATON

Published in Great Britain 2015
by Mills & Boon, an imprint of Harlequin (UK) Limited,
Eton House, 18-24 Paradise Road, Richmond, Surrey, TW9 1SR

© 2015 Louisa Heaton

ISBN: 978-0-263-24702-2

Harlequin (UK) Limited's policy is to use papers that are natural,
renewable and recyclable products and made from wood grown in
sustainable forests. The logging and manufacturing processes conform
to the legal environmental regulations of the country of origin.

Printed and bound in Spain
by CPI, Barcelona

Louisa Heaton first started writing romance at school, and would take her stories in to show her friends, scrawled in a big red binder, with plenty of crossing out. She dreamt of romance herself, and after knowing her husband-to-be for only three weeks shocked her parents by accepting his marriage proposal. After four children—including a set of twins—and fifteen years of trying to get published, she finally received 'The Call'! Now she lives on Hayling Island, and when she's not busy as a First Responder creates her stories wandering along the wonderful Hampshire coastline with her two dogs, muttering to herself and scaring the locals.

Visit Louisa on twitter @louisaheaton, on Facebook www.facebook.com/Louisaheatonauthor or on her website: www.louisaheaton.com

Books by Louisa Heaton

The Baby That Changed Her Life

**Visit the author profile page
at millsandboon.co.uk for more titles**

For MJ and Honey x

CHAPTER ONE

Dr Oliver James was just packing up for the day when his father, Patrick, put his head round the door.

'Got a minute?'

Olly looked up, his bright blue eyes curious. 'Yeah, sure. What's up?'

His father was the senior GP at their practice in the village of Atlee Wold, although not for long. He was taking early retirement, and he'd hired a locum to fill his space until a more permanent doctor could be found.

'That new locum I told you about. She's here. I thought I'd introduce you.'

Right. The new locum. It was a day he was dreading—his father stepping down and away from the practice—and the arrival of a locum brought that day another step closer.

And he was exhausted. It had been a long, cold day. With all the snow outside, it had taken a long time for his consulting room to warm up and he'd spent his time in between seeing patients sipping hot tea and leaning against the ancient radiators. What he really wanted, more than anything else, was to go home and take a long, hot shower and maybe not emerge until he could summon up the energy to get dry and fall into bed. Perhaps with a mug of cocoa?

But even a shower wasn't on the night's agenda, because it was his turn to be on call. Which meant a night trying to sleep fully dressed on his bed, ready to pull his shoes on if his pager sounded. Oh, and a coat, of course, with a scarf and a woolly hat and gloves. And hoping to hell that his old four-wheel drive started up.

'Is she here? I didn't know she was coming today?'

'Well, she's not *here*, exactly. She's at the village hall, running a class.'

Olly raised his eyebrows, impressed. 'She's not been here five minutes. How is she running a *class*?' What was she? Wonder Woman?

His father laughed. 'When she came for her interview she put up flyers. Haven't you seen them? Belly-dancing classes at the village hall? All ages, both sexes welcome.'

Olly smirked. '*Belly dancing?* She'll be lucky if anyone turns up to *that*. The old dears round here consider knitting to be their only exercise, and the men their hanging baskets. Can't imagine any of them shaking their wobbly bits in the village hall. Besides, it's freezing.'

'Well, I said we'd pop in, show our support, and it will give you two the opportunity to meet. You'll be working together for a while—until I get a permanent replacement.'

There it was again. The harsh reminder that his father was *leaving*. That things were *changing*. That he had no say in it.

'She doesn't want to do it?'

He didn't quite understand locums. Why travel from one place to another, never really staying anywhere, never getting to know people? Why didn't they just put some roots down somewhere? He knew he'd hate it if it were him.

'She's not sure. But she wants to give the place a trial run.'

'Shouldn't *we* be the ones to offer *her* the trial run?'

Olly was quite territorial about their practice. It had been in the James family for some time. His own father, and Patrick's father, Dermot, had run it before him. The fact that his father had sought a *female* locum also annoyed him.

His father was probably trying to matchmake again. Find Olly a wife, who would then provide them all with the next line of doctors for the village of Atlee Wold.

'We can but see. She's a charming girl. I think you'll like her,' his father said, with a twinkle in his eyes that was obvious in its implication.

'Dad, you'd make an awful Cupid.'

His father frowned in wry amusement, his brow furrowing into long lines across his weathered forehead. 'Why?'

'Because the wings wouldn't suit you and I'm not sure I'd want to trust you with a bow and arrow.'

'Don't know what you mean. Besides, you've got no worries there, son. She won't match any of the criteria on your "perfect wife" list.'

Olly laughed. Everyone joked about his list. Even if he didn't. There was a serious point to it, after all. If a woman were to be his wife, then she'd need particular qualities. The wife of a country doctor had to have certain standards. Respectability, loyalty, charm, an inner beauty and a calm head on a solid pair of shoulders. Someone who could hold the fort and rear the children. Okay, it might make him seem a bit Victorian in his thinking, but what was wrong with wanting a dependable woman?

'Good. I'd hate to think you were Cupid in disguise. Like I said, with your eyesight the arrows could end up anywhere.'

Patrick helped his son pack up, switch off all the lights and then make sure his call bag was stocked with anything he might need for the night. Then, despite the snow, despite the cold, and despite his tiredness, Patrick and Olly got into Olly's four-wheel drive and set off for the village hall.

It really wasn't very far. Less than a mile. But the snow was thick and still falling. The towns and busy roads in the cities might have grit and salt, but here in Atlee Wold, a Hampshire backwater, they seemed to be lacking everything except table salt from the village shop, which the locals had put out. Some had even put out kitty litter to grit their pathways. Those that were able to shovelled the pathways of those that weren't.

Theirs was a strong community, where people helped each other out where they could. But Olly really hadn't expected that there would be nowhere for him to park in the village hall car park! Or that the pathway would be so well trampled by the many feet that had passed that he could actually see the pavement.

Or that there'd be the beat and throb of loud exotic music clearly heard from some distance away.

'Well, I'll be…'

He parked his four-wheel drive by a tall hedge and when he pushed open his car door to get out it sent down a spray of snow on top of him. Some of it went down the back of his neck and top and he shivered as the icy crystals tickled his spine.

'Ugh!'

Patrick laughed. 'Looks like a full house.'

'You don't have to be so delighted.'

The village hall was lit along its gutters with old Christmas lights that hadn't yet been taken down, and from the windows bright yellow light flared. There was the sound of Indian music, loud but muffled, emanating from the building itself, with an earthy beat.

Olly shook his head with disbelief. How had a complete stranger managed to rabble-rouse an entire village to do belly dancing? He might have expected the hall to be full if it was a gardening class or crochet, bingo or a knitting circle, but *belly dancing*?

Part of him just couldn't wait to meet this Wonder Woman. An image of her was building in his head. She was a GP, so she had to be somewhat sensible. Someone middle-aged and quite strait-laced who did belly dancing because it was just something different? Perhaps she had to fight for attention and this was her way… As his father said, *not* a woman to threaten his list of the attributes a 'perfect wife' ought to have.

Belly-dancing instructor was nowhere on the list at all!

Shaking the snow from his shoulders, he entered the village hall after his father. There was a small foyer that they went into first, with a tuck shop to one side. Then there were two large rooms in the village hall and one was in darkness. From the other the music blared.

'You ready?' His father had to raise his voice to be heard.

'Of course I am!' he called back, pulling open the door.

But he stopped in his tracks when he saw the woman leading the class. His dad even bumped into him from behind.

Olly gaped open-mouthed at the new locum GP.

This is not what I expected.

She was petite—elfin, almost—with a graceful, slim, but womanly figure which he couldn't help but notice due to her clothing. Or what there was of it. Her dark, almost black hair was cut short at the back, but at the front it was long and multicoloured—cyan blue, purple and pink streaks fell across her face. Her arms were layered with bangles and she had a red jewel in her belly button and she twirled and swirled and sashayed as she led the class in 'undulation one'.

'All right, Olly?' his dad asked, staring at his son in amusement.

How can this woman be a GP? She doesn't look like one.

But what was a GP *supposed* to look like? There was a shimmery wrap around her waist, tightly sheathing her perfectly curved bottom, and it tinkled and glimmered as she moved. Then, as she pointed her tiny feet, he noticed tattoos and nail polish and toe rings, before his eyes rose back up to her face to see large brown eyes, rosy cheeks and a cheeky smile.

Patrick leaned in closer to his son to whisper in his ear. 'Close your mouth. You look like a hungry hippo.'

Olly did as he was told and swallowed hard. This wasn't a GP. She looked like a pixie. An imp. Or a fairy. Yes, that was it—a fairy.

If she turns around I'll see she's got wings on her back.

But there were no wings. Just another tattoo. He couldn't make out what it was from this distance…

And the hall was full! Here were people and patients that he knew well. People who suffered from arthritis and hip problems and knee problems. And here they all were, shaking their booty with the best of them, smiles plastered across their faces.

They must be off their meds.

Or their heads.

One of his patients, Mrs Macabee, noticed him from her position midway down the class. 'Ooh, hello, Dr James! Fancy seeing you here! Are you joining us?'

He watched Mrs Macabee tilt her hip up and down, up and down. He blinked his head to clear the image, remembered what he was there for and then smiled politely. 'Sorry, Mrs M, I don't dance—and besides, I'm here on business.' He had to raise his voice to be heard.

'This is *business*?' She laughed as she followed their new GP in her instructions.

He simply couldn't believe it. Here was half the village, packing out the small hall—young and old, self-respect be damned, all kitted out with hip scarves and coin-edged skirts, shaking their backsides and waving their arms about.

The music was catchy, though, and he was unaware that his foot had been tapping to the beat until it suddenly stopped and everyone started clapping each other. Their new GP was thanking everyone for coming…patting herself down with a soft, pink towel.

There were lots of people fighting over each other to go to her and thank her for so much fun, the best time they'd had in ages, et cetera, et cetera.

Olly pursed his lips as he waited for everyone to file out after handing back their belly-dancing garb. He nodded hello at a lot of them.

His father looked bemused. 'Why are you smiling so much?' he asked his old man.

'It's the look on your face.'

'What's wrong with it?'

Patrick laughed. 'What's *right* with it? You look like you've been sucking lemons.'

'Don't be ridiculous.'

His father was being silly. Of course he didn't look that way. Why would he? That would imply that he was jealous of this woman or something, wouldn't it? And he had nothing to be jealous of! So she'd got the village out to an exercise class… So what?

The pixie came over, towelling her face dry. 'Hi!'

She was still full of energy, it seemed, and appeared quite happy with the way the class had gone.

His father stepped forward to make the introductions. 'Lula—this is my son, Oliver. Olly, this is Dr Lula Chance.'

He held out his hand to shake hers, aware of how much the bangles jingled as he did so. 'Lula? That's an odd name—where's that from?'

'It's short for Louise. I prefer Lula. Like hula.'

He looked at her bare slim waist and womanly curves. 'And do you?' he asked, dragging his eyes back up to her face.

'Do I what?'

He swallowed hard. 'Hula?'

She beamed a dazzling smile in his direction and it was like being smacked in the gut.

'I've been known to.'

She was patting her chest with the towel, attracting the attention of his gaze, and he had to fight *really hard* to keep his eyes on her face.

'So you're the guy with the list?'

Olly's cheeks coloured—and not from the cold. 'I am. Nothing's private here, it would seem. Welcome to village life.'

Patrick laughed and laid a hand on Lula's shoulder. 'Well done, Lula! Getting everyone out like that! Your class seemed a success!'

She nodded, her blue, purple and pink fringe quivering around her face. 'I hope so. The first class was free, to get people interested. The real test is in seeing if they come back and pay for it.'

'The real test is making sure none of them have a heart attack. Have you got oxygen on standby?' Olly asked.

Patrick laughed at his son. 'I'm sure they'll be fine. Now—to business. Have you moved in yet?'

'My boxes are in the car. You've got the key to the cottage?'

Olly looked up, his sulk gone. 'Which cottage?'

She frowned. 'Erm…Moonrose Cottage, I think it's called. Is that right, Patrick?'

Patrick? She's calling him Patrick? What happened to Dr James?

'Moonrose? You're moving into *Gran's* old cottage?'

His father looked at him sternly. 'Yes, she is—and you're going to help her.' He handed over the key.

His dad *knew* how he felt about Moonrose Cottage! It might be his gran's old place, but it was also where his own mother had grown up. The place had special memories. If they let it out to this pixie then God only knew what she'd fill it with. Parties, or raves, or something equally mad. Moonrose was a quiet, sedate house. Charming and conservative and quintessentially English.

'But I'm on call.'

'And Lula, here, has offered to be on call with you whilst you help her unpack.' He grinned. 'Isn't that kind of her?'

Olly looked at Lula and raised an eyebrow at those large brown eyes twinkling madly at him and doing weird things to his stomach and other body parts.

'It is. Thank you, Lula. Though you must be tired—travelling, running a dance class, moving in, going on call?'

'I like to pack a lot into life.' She dabbed at her chest with the towel and again he had to concentrate really hard not to look.

'You don't say?'

Patrick stepped away. 'Well, I'll leave you two to it. Olly, I'll walk back home— it's not far. You go on with Lula and I'll see you both in the morning.'

He shook Lula's hand and then waved goodbye and stepped out, leaving Olly and Lula alone.

Olly felt uncomfortable. There were no women like Lula in Atlee Wold. Vivid and bright and crazy and...

And what?

'So, Moonrose Cottage, eh?' He stared at her hair. So many colours...like a rainbow.

'Yeah... Strange name, I thought.'

'It's after the Blue Moon roses my gran planted when she was a little girl. They're all around it and they won prizes in the village show. If you're still here in summer you'll see them in bloom. They're quite beautiful.'

She smiled. 'I'm sure they are.'

'So, shall I give you a hand to pack all this bling away?' He pointed at the box full of coin-edged skirts and multicoloured scarves she'd given to his patients.

Lula laughed. 'Thanks. It *is* a lot of bling. The hall warden said I could store it below the stage.'

'Okay.'

He helped her lift a large bag through the stage door opening. They were about to leave when Lula pointed out a couple of boxes covered by thick blankets.

'Could you help me take those out? They're mine. I couldn't leave them in the car.'

Olly nodded and hefted the two boxes one on top of the other, hearing metal clank inside. Then they left the village hall, pulling the door closed after switching off the lights.

Outside, the snow was lit by the fairy lights, so it blinked softly in reds and blues, yellows and greens. It was really quite pretty, and had the effect of making Lula look even more multicoloured than she had been before. Like a peacock.

Definitely a magical fairy.

'Are you okay?' she asked.

He blinked. 'Sorry?'

'You were staring. At me.' She grinned.

Olly licked his lips, thinking quickly. 'Ah, right…yes. Erm…I was just wondering where you'd parked your car? I don't see one.'

She pointed, her hand seeming to twinkle in the lights as they reflected off her rings and bangles. 'I parked down the road. I wanted the patients to be able to park close.'

'That's kind.'

She accepted the compliment. 'Thank you. I try to be. So…?'

'So…?'

'Will you drive in front? Show me where the cottage is?'

Of course! Idiot! Stupid!

'Sure. But let's make sure your car starts first.'

'Oh, she always does.'

'She?'

'Betsy.'

'Your car is called Betsy?'

'Betsy the Bug.' She stopped in front of a red car with large black polka dots on it, like a ladybird.

Once again Olly was left standing mute and blinking. After a moment he managed, 'Cute.'

'I think so. Here—why don't you put that large one in the front? This small one can go in the boot.'

Her engine rumbled into life straight away and he pointed out his four-wheel drive, further up the road. Lula said that she'd wait for him and he walked back up to his car, his boots crunching in the snow, muttering to himself.

'Dad, I'm going to kill you... What on earth have you done?'

As a choice of locum she was a tad...out there. Not the sort of locum he'd expected his father to hire. There had to have been plenty of other doctors he might have chosen from. Sensible, sedate people. The type to blend in with village life.

Not this firecracker...

His four-wheel drive started first time and he indicated to pull out, noticing her following him through the high street. He took a left and kept looking in his rearview mirror to make sure she was still there. Still following.

He thought of his 'perfect wife' list.

She didn't match any of the items on it.

But he felt mysteriously intrigued by her.

Bewitching. That's what she is.

Lula followed Olly through the village roads, realizing she'd made a big mistake. When she'd come for her interview with Patrick, she'd known she was getting involved with a father-and-son team and that had seemed fine. But Patrick was a silver-haired fox, with sparkling, kind eyes, and she should have just *known* that the son was going to be drop-dead gorgeous. However, she hadn't worried too much about it. She'd concentrated much more on her other reason for coming to Atlee Wold and assumed that Patrick's son would be just another person to work with.

But when he'd walked into that village hall… It had been as if a film star had walked in. She'd half expected to see paparazzi following him in. Gorgeous and sexy, yet a down-to-earth guy. She'd tried to ignore him so that she could carry on with her class. She'd even stumbled over her steps. But thankfully no one had seemed to notice.

And now she was following him. Through the snowy streets. In Betsy. Following his old jalopy.

Olly had pulled up outside a small thatched cottage surrounded by tall briar wood. It looked pretty, and she could only imagine how gorgeous it might look in the summertime, with its white walls and blue roses, butterflies and bees flitting about the place. There was an arched trellis over the front door, with what looked like an ancient Russian vine growing over it.

It really wasn't that far from the GP surgery, or the village hall, and she hoped that tomorrow she could try walking in to work. She had a pair of wellies somewhere in one of the boxes she already had in the car. A small removals lorry would drop off her other stuff tomorrow.

He stood back so she could make fresh tracks in the snow to the front door, and then he passed her a key.

Smiling, she took it and tried to reassure him. 'Don't worry—I'll look after the place.'

'I'm sure you will. Shall we get the lights on, the fire burning and then get your boxes in?'

Lula nodded. 'Sounds great.' Though it might be a bit awkward, the two of them alone before a roaring fire…

The key turned easily and she pushed open the door, wondering what to expect. Patrick had agreed to let the cottage out to her at a reduced rate and the price was very reasonable. She certainly wouldn't be able to get a place in London at the rate he'd given her—not even a bedsit! And here she was with the key to a beautiful, thatched, two-bedroom cottage.

Inside, she found the light switches and gasped in delight. The low roof created an immediate intimacy in the small rooms. The lounge furniture was covered in white sheets, but when she removed them she found old, chintzy chairs, with scatter cushions made from patchwork, and an old green leather sofa. The walls were whitewashed, with exposed dark beams, and there was a good-sized fireplace already stacked with logs.

'Shall I start the fire for you?' Olly said.

Lula smiled. 'That's okay. I can do it. Why don't you get me those boxes from Betsy?'

He nodded, but she could tell he would have been a lot happier playing with the fire.

Typical man.

She liked Olly already. He was charming and old-fashioned and very English. He had classic good looks, with dark blond hair and bright blue eyes like Chris Hemsworth. *Just my type.* But, despite the handsome looks and the knockout body, she hoped she didn't have to worry about there being an attraction between them whilst they worked. It wasn't the sort of thing she was looking for. Not here. There were other reasons for her being in Atlee Wold and romance wasn't one of them.

The firelighters worked quickly and Lula soon had a bright orange flame licking at the wood. There was a stack of old newspapers to one side, and she screwed up a few and inserted them into gaps in the wood to help it. Soon the crackling flames had taken hold and the fire began to build. She stood warming her hands as Olly came barging in, carrying the larger of her two blanketed boxes.

'What's *in* this thing?'

She took it from him, looked around and saw a table in the corner that looked suitable. Setting the box down, she freed the blanket and whipped it off. 'Say hello to Nefertiti and Cleo!'

She saw him take a step back, his mouth open in shock and horror. 'Are they...*rats*?'

Lula grinned and bit her lip as she stooped down to open the door of the cage and both rats—one dark brown and one pure white with pink eyes—climbed out onto her hands and ran up her arm to sit on her shoulder. 'Dumbo rats. Aren't they beautiful?'

He looked carefully at her, as if judging her sanity. 'They're *rats*.'

'They're very intelligent animals.'

'So are dolphins, but you don't have two of those, do you?' He watched the rats play around under the dark wisps of Lula's hair, their noses and whiskers twitching. Then he had a sudden dreadful thought. 'What's in the other box? The one in the boot of your car?'

Lula grinned. 'Anubis. You'd better get him—he's on a heat pad especially.'

Olly put his hands on his hips. '*What* is Anubis?'

She tilted her head to one side, amused by his reaction. 'I'll get him. Here.'

She reached up and took hold of the two rats from under her hair and planted them on his shoulder. She could see how he froze and winced and twitched at each of their movements as they gave him a good sniff. Their little pink noses and whiskers tickled his ears.

Olly stood frozen, as if rigor mortis had set in. 'Please hurry.'

Lula chuckled, threw her jacket on and rushed out into the snow. Pretty soon she came back with the smaller blanketed box and put it on the coffee table. There was a cable and plug for this one, and when she pressed the wall switch a small light came on inside the blanket.

Olly stood awkwardly with the two rats running about his shoulders. 'Could you take these?'

Lula laughed. He looked so funny standing there, with his shoulders all hunched up by his ears and two rats perched on his shoulder, trying to sniff the hair on his head. She scooped them up easily and placed them back in their cage.

Olly let out a big breath and then brushed off his shoulders. 'Thanks. So, Anubis…what is he?'

She looked at him slightly askance. 'He's my big challenge.'

'Challenge? Why?'

'Because I'm scared to death of him, and as I'm determined to beat all my fears I've borrowed him from a friend until I get over that fear.'

Olly gave a single nod. 'And that fear is called…?' Though he had a suspicion.

Lula removed the blanket. 'Arachnophobia.'

In the small tank, amongst some wood and soil, was a large, very dark, very hairy, red-kneed tarantula.

He peered closer. 'It's bigger than my hand.'

'Isn't he a beauty?'

'I thought you were scared?'

'I am. But I can still appreciate how gorgeous he is.'

'And it's your aim in life to pick this thing up?'

She nodded. 'One of my aims. Eventually.'

Olly shook his head. 'You're madder than a boxful of circus clowns.'

They both laughed, but then Lula shivered and headed over to the fire and stood with her back to it, hands stretched out behind her. 'Freezing!'

'Shall I get the rest of the boxes?'

'If you wouldn't mind?'

'It depends… Are there any more zoo creatures in Betsy?'

Lula smiled. 'Just woolly jumpers.'

'Safe enough. Though you might have warned me earlier that I was handling livestock.'

They'd unloaded all the boxes, and Lula had put her clothes away and freshened up, when Olly's phone rang. The out-of-hours doctor service informed him that one of his older patients in the area was suffering from chest pains. Could he go?

'It's Mr Maynard. He lives out on one of the farms. We'll take my car.'

Lula nodded. It would be best to start with, until she got to know her way around—where the best roads were, what shortcuts there were. And this was a good way to meet some of the patients who couldn't make it into the surgery for various reasons. She was particularly drawn to find all of those patients who tried to keep themselves hidden away and make sure she saw *everyone*.

As Olly drove he filled her in on Mr Maynard.

'He's eighty-two years old and lives alone. His farm was a dairy once, but he never married or had kids and during the nineties everything just fell to pieces. He had to sell his herd and now he lives in the farmhouse alone.'

Lula thought it sounded a very lonely existence. 'How does he get out and about?'

'He doesn't. His arthritis is bad, so he doesn't drive. Molly from the village shop goes up twice a week with his shopping and drops it into his kitchen. He generally looks after himself.'

'Any other health conditions I ought to know about?'

'He's got high blood pressure, but he's on medication for that.'

'Ramipril?'

Olly nodded. 'And a diuretic.'

The diuretic had been included to help reduce fluid in the body. The more fluid there was to be transported in thin arteries, the higher the blood pressure, so a diuretic helped to reduce fluid build-up.

Driving through the village at night was quite surreal. Everywhere was covered in snow, and yellow lamplight lit the way every thirty yards or so, until eventually they hit the outskirts of the village and the lamplight disappeared. They had to rely on the four-wheel drive's headlights, and with thick snow still falling it was very slow going.

Lula wondered how on earth Molly at the shop would even get to Mr Maynard's farm with the ground covered like this. Did she have a four-wheel drive?

A sign appeared—'Burner's Farm'—and Olly turned into its driveway. They were bumped and jostled along as he drove down the pitted road and eventually an old stone farmhouse appeared, surrounded by old barns and out-buildings in a crumbling state of decay. It was hard to see the property's true state at night, but Lula could see that there were sections of roof missing from the barn due to the snowfall, and that all the old machinery was decaying from lack of use.

Alighting from the car, Olly grabbed his bag and he and Lula trudged through the snow to the farmhouse door. Olly banged on it quite hard, before pushing it open and calling out. 'Mr Maynard? Donald? It's Dr James and Dr Chance.'

'In here,' a croaky voice called back.

The hallway was dark, but at the end of it was a brightly lit room from which warmth poured. Lula was glad he had a coal fire on the go, and was keeping warm at least. Their patient was sitting in a chair with blankets round him, and at his side were the remains of a hot dinner and a glass of red wine.

'Donald? This is Dr Chance—she's new at the surgery. How are you?'

Mr Maynard peered past Olly at her and beamed in a giant smile. 'Well, hello, dear, and what a pretty little thing you are!'

'Hello, Mr Maynard. How are you doing?' She sat down beside him, instantly taking in whatever information she could—the colour of his skin, whether or not he seemed clammy, his respiratory rate—but he looked good. He was a healthy colour, not out of breath and with no signs of sweating.

'I'm all right now. They just panic at the other end of the phone, don't they?'

She felt sure he was referring to the people who manned the out-of-hours doctor service. She herself didn't think they panicked, but they had to respond urgently if a patient mentioned chest pains. It could be life-threatening.

'What made you call in tonight?'

'Well, my chest was hurting, my dear, and when you're all alone you convince yourself you're about to kick the bucket at any moment so I rang up. But I had a damned good belch and felt a lot better. Just indigestion, I think—all stuff and nonsense. No need for you to have come out and checked on me.'

She shook her head, smiling, and patted the back of his hand. 'There's every need to check on you. Now, while we're here, let's check your blood pressure and pulse—is that okay?'

He let them do their tests, and he seemed quite well. His blood pressure was in the normal range for him and his pulse rate was steady and strong. He had no pain, and they could see that he'd eaten a particularly strong curry, so perhaps he was right and it *was* just indigestion he'd experienced.

'You're on your own out here, Mr Maynard?' Lula asked.

'Call me Donald, dear.'

'Donald.' She smiled.

'I am. Been this way for years—lost my Teddy eight years back.'

'Teddy?'

'The dog,' Olly said. 'Gorgeous Border collie, he was.'

'That he was,' said Donald.

'Don't you miss getting out and about, Donald? You must get bored, being here in these four walls all the time?'

'I do…but what am I going to do? I don't like bingo, and I don't like going down the pub—it's not my thing. I like a bit of culture, me, and there ain't no culture in Atlee Wold.'

Lula nodded in understanding. 'You like wine?' She pointed at his glass.

'Only the good stuff!' He chuckled.

'Well, you leave it with me, Donald. Let me see what I can arrange.'

When they got back in the car Olly looked at her questioningly. 'What are you planning?'

'I know someone who knows someone else. I think we can get Mr Maynard out and about and enjoying life again. Why should he be stuck at that farm with just memories? There's life in the old dog yet.'

He smiled. 'He seemed to like you.'

'He's a nice guy.'

'He *is* a nice guy. But I've been trying to get him involved with village life for years and he's never budged from that chair.'

She smiled mysteriously. 'Perhaps he needs something more than just this village? Never underestimate the power of a good woman.'

He looked at her askance. What was wrong with 'just' the village?

Perhaps she bewitches her patients, too.

* * *

The next morning Lula telephoned a colleague's friend in Petersfield, who ran coach holidays, and told him about Donald Maynard. After a quick discussion they found a trip for Donald that they thought would suit him down to the ground. It was a tour of wineries in the Loire region of France, over three days, stopping off at some lovely B & Bs along the way and all at a greatly reduced price.

Lula rang Mr Maynard and asked him if he could be ready in a week's time to catch a bus, if it collected him from the end of his driveway.

Donald was thrilled. 'Chuffed to mint balls' was his expression, and he couldn't thank Lula enough. She put the phone down at her end, feeling delighted that she'd been able to help a wonderful old man who deserved to enjoy life, despite his years.

She got herself ready for work. Determined to walk to the surgery, she rooted around for her wellies. With her woolly hat and scarf on, she was ready to go, and she opened her door, expecting to set straight off. She wanted to make a good impression on her very first day at the surgery.

But someone had left a cardboard box on her doorstep.

And inside something was crying.

CHAPTER TWO

LULA TOOK A sharp intake of breath in the cold morning air. There had been no more snow after their trip home from Mr Maynard's farm last night, and the top layer had frozen to a crisp. The cardboard box was from a biscuit manufacturer, and the top had all four corners folded into each other, with some air holes punched through by something like a ballpoint pen.

Lula almost couldn't believe her eyes.

This sort of thing didn't happen twice in a lifetime…

Kneeling down, she peeled back the corners and looked inside to see a newly born baby, swaddled in tight blankets and towels.

'Oh, my God!'

Lula scooped up the baby and stood up, holding it to her, undoing her coat buttons and scooting the baby inside her greatcoat. Beneath the baby there was a blue hot water bottle, and it was still quite warm, so Lula could only hope that the baby hadn't been left outside in the cold for too long. With her free hand she picked up the cardboard box and brought it inside, kicking the door closed, then she went back over to the fire to add more logs and get it really going again.

When that was done she picked up her phone and dialled the police. There was no police station in Atlee Wold itself, but there was one in the next village over—South Wold. She could only assume they'd send someone from there.

She wanted to examine the baby, but the need to keep it warm and monitor its breathing overrode all other instincts. Next she called the surgery, assuming one of the receptionists would answer, but Olly did.

'Atlee Surgery.'

His voice was solid and reassuring to hear.

'Oliver?'

'Lula? What's up?'

'You need to come over.'

'I'm about to start morning surgery.'

'Can your father do it? I need you here. Now.'

He paused for a moment, but he must have been swayed by the quiet desperation in her voice because he said, 'I'll be right over.'

Lula paced the floor—back and forth, back and forth—humming tunes, gently jigging the baby up and down, trying to keep it monitored, checking on its breathing. She had no idea if it was a boy or a girl, or even if it had all its bits and pieces—there'd been no time to check. When Olly got there maybe they could check the baby together.

Suddenly she remembered she ought to have asked him to bring his call-out bag, and hoped he'd have heard from her tone that it might be needed.

Why didn't I tell him it was needed? So stupid!

Because the shock of finding the baby had been so great. It wasn't what you expected to find when you went out through the front door in the morning. At the most you might expect a present from the cat, if you kept one, or perhaps a friendly offering from a night-time fox on your doorstep. But a baby…?

No.

She knew what would happen. The police would arrive, and they'd take everything. The baby, the blankets, the hot water bottle, the box. They'd try and trace its mother, but it would be difficult. There were never enough clues in this sort of situation, even if the mother left a note...

She rummaged in the box.

No note.

Where's the mother?

More importantly, *who* was the mother? She had to have been desperate to do this. To leave her baby in a cardboard box, in the middle of winter, on the doorstep of a stranger. She couldn't have known that the baby would be found early. Could she? What if Lula had been on a late shift? The baby would have frozen to death. It didn't bear thinking about.

It might be a teenage girl—someone afraid to tell her parents that she'd been pregnant. But how would you hide something like that? The baby looked a decent size—about seven pounds. It was obviously full term, so the pregnancy must have shown.

Perhaps it was an older woman who'd had an affair, and then her husband had come back from Afghanistan, or somewhere, and she'd had to get rid of it?

No, Lula, too far-fetched.

Or was it?

Finding a baby on her doorstep would probably have sounded too far-fetched yesterday.

There was a hammering on her front door and she rushed over to open it, letting Olly in. He stopped and stared at the baby and she saw the puzzlement on his face.

'It's not mine!'

'Where did it come from?' He closed the door behind him, pulling off his jacket.

She explained what had happened and they laid the baby on the rug in front of the roaring fire to examine it.

She was newborn. Barely hours old. The umbilical cord was tied off with navy blue string and still fresh. Vernix—

the grease that covered a baby in the womb, to stop its skin getting waterlogged—was in the armpits and creases of the baby, indicating that maybe she was a little before term.

She was a little cold, but otherwise well.

She was extremely lucky.

'She can't have been outside long,' Olly said.

'Perhaps she'd only just been left by someone?'

'Did you see anyone when you went outside? When you opened the door?'

Lula tried to think. But the shock of finding an abandoned baby had overridden everything. She couldn't recall looking around the cottage or past the garden. She'd noticed the box, heard the crying and snuffling, and when she'd seen it was a baby had hurried back inside.

'I didn't look.'

'Lula…'

'I didn't *think*! I was in shock! I…you don't expect this, do you?' She wrapped the baby up again and scooped her up, holding her tight against her body.

Olly watched her pace back and forth. 'There must be a mother somewhere. She could be at risk if she doesn't get proper medical attention.'

She nodded. 'I know. I figure it has to be a teenager. Who do you know in the village that fits the bill?'

Olly sank onto the couch. 'There are a few teenagers in the village—about twenty or so, I think. Most of them catch the school bus to go to the comprehensive in South Wold. I don't see them very much—they don't tend to come and see the doctor.'

'Have any come to you about going on the pill? Any who you think could be sexually active?'

He shook his head. 'No. I honestly haven't seen any for a while. I think the last teenager I saw was the Blakes's daughter, and that was for an ear infection.'

He racked his brains, but Olly could think of no one

he'd seen at the surgery lately. Nor had he seen any teenage girl about the village on his day-to-day travels who had aroused his suspicion.

Surely he would have noticed a pregnant teenager?

But, then again, the same could be said for the girl's parents. How did you *not* notice?

Olly made them both a drink, cringing at the sight of Anubis on the kitchen counter. All darkness and legs.

He'd just taken the tea through to the lounge when the police arrived.

There was a lot of questioning, a lot of hustle and bustle. Lula gave a statement, and then Olly told them the little he knew—that he couldn't think of anyone who might have been concealing a pregnancy.

Lula felt quite protective of the little mite, and almost didn't want to hand her over, but in the end she did, her heart sinking a little at the thought of what the future might hold for the little girl. Would she get lost in the system? Be passed from family to family?

She could only hope that they would find the baby's mother. Before it was too late.

After the police had gone, and the small lounge and kitchen had emptied of uniformed bodies, she sank down into the seat by the fire and stared at Olly, ignoring the way the firelight flickered in the reflection of his blue eyes.

'What a welcome to the village!'

He attempted a smile. 'We did what we could for her.'

'I worry that it's not enough. Poor thing.'

'We'll find the mum.'

'But what if we *don't*? That baby will enter the system and there's no guarantee of a happy ending for her, you know? Not all foster homes are great.'

He cocked his head to one side. 'Are you speaking from experience?'

She met his gaze, noticing how beautiful his dark blue

eyes were, framed by thick dark lashes. Men could be so lucky with their eyelashes, it seemed.

Lula nodded, deciding to be open with him. 'I was like that little baby once. But I wasn't left in a cardboard box in the snow in the middle of winter. My mother left me in a Moses basket on a beach.'

'You were abandoned?' He sat forward.

She gave a wry smile. 'From what I know, I was found by a family who were packing up their beach hut. They'd been with their kids by the water's edge, paddling and stuff. When they came back they found me. My mother had left a note, saying how sorry she was, how much she regretted doing it, but that she couldn't keep me. With the note was this.' She reached into her neckline and pulled out a silver necklace with a heart charm on the end. 'She signed the note with the initials "EL".'

'"EL"? That's all you were left with?'

'And that she'd called me Louise.' Lula sipped her drink and smiled at him. 'You don't have to feel sorry for me, you know. I've lived my life to the full.'

'It's not over yet. You've got years left.'

'We never know, though, do we? I could get knocked down by a bus tomorrow.'

He frowned. 'Actually, you couldn't. There's no bus service tomorrow.'

She smiled, but then Olly was serious again. 'What happened to you?'

Lula shrugged. 'I went from home to home till I was about seven and then I got put with a family who decided they wanted to adopt me.'

'The Chances?'

'Yes. They were lovely—really sweet people—but I knew I didn't belong to them.'

'They'd chosen you. Out of all those children looking

for a permanent home, they picked *you*. You should be pleased about that.'

'They had other adopted children and each of them had a problem, too. A health problem. Peter and Daisy Chance seemed to go after all the hard-luck cases—don't ask me why.'

'Perhaps they thought that children with issues needed the most love?'

She shrugged. 'Maybe.'

'But what was wrong with *you*? If you don't mind me asking?'

She smiled. 'I had leukaemia. Childhood leukaemia. They had no idea if I was going to live or die, and still the Chances wanted me. That was pretty brave of them, huh?'

He nodded, thoughtful.

'I got better—though the chemo did some horrible things.'

'But you got through it okay?'

'As okay as I could at that age.'

Olly smiled. 'You seem well now, though, and—as you say yourself—you pack everything into life. You work as a doctor, which is hard work and stressful, and you do other stuff, too.'

'I made the decision to be happy and enjoy life and take my medicine every day.' She smiled at him.

He looked at her strangely and she laughed at the curious frown on his face. 'Why are you laughing?'

'It was your face!' She chuckled.

'Thanks. A man likes to know his looks are amusing.'

'It's not your looks, Olly. There's nothing wrong with those. But it was the way you *looked* at me.'

'I was admiring you,' he protested. 'I mean, I was admiring your *attitude* to life. Not admiring *you*, per se. Not with that hair,' he added with a wry grin.

She pursed her lips with amusement and then stood up

and looked in the mirror over the fireplace. 'There's nothing wrong with my hair.' She checked some of the strands, tweaking and rearranging her colours.

He stood up next to her and they both looked at each other in the mirror's reflection. 'No, of course not—it's very…conservative.'

'Hah! Now you're being a snob. I thought I might add another colour to it, actually.'

'Really?' He raised his eyebrows in question.

'What do you think to making the rest of it green?'

'You can't be serious?'

'I'm deadly serious.'

He opened his mouth to say something, but nothing came out. His open-mouthed flustering made her burst into more laughter and she punched him playfully on the arm. 'I'm just joshing with you. Of course I'm not going green.'

'Thank God for that!'

'I was thinking more like letter-box red.'

He didn't believe her this time. He picked up his jacket and threw it on. 'Well, though it has been fun, Dr Chance, deciding whether you want to look like your head has been in a collision with a paint factory, you and I need to put in an appearance at work. Otherwise the whole village may well fall foul of a deadly plague without our being in our chairs, ministering to the sick.'

'Hmm… I'm not one to turn down the chance of fighting an epidemic.'

'Ready to go, then?'

She put on her own coat and the incredibly long scarf that she'd been wearing earlier. 'As I'll ever be.'

'You don't need to feed the animals before we go?'

'Already done.'

'Any closer to picking up Anubis?' He meant the tarantula.

'No. But I gave him a damned good look this morning, and I got within two feet of the tank without shaking.'

'Progress!'

'Exactly!'

'Do you want to sit in with me this morning? We could do the clinic together and it would give me the opportunity to fill you in on some of our frequent flyers.'

He meant the regulars who always turned up to the surgery, no matter what the state of their health. Every surgery had them. They were the people you could depend upon to turn up, who had nothing wrong with them but had got themselves appointments because they were lonely, or they wanted to chat about their problems in life in general.

Then there were the hypochondriacs, who turned up over every little niggle—real or imagined. But you had to take them seriously each time, and check them out no matter what, or you'd get *The Boy Who Cried Wolf* syndrome. If one day you decided to ignore their call for help it would be the one time that they were actually ill and really needed you.

'Sure. I think that would be a good idea.'

'And if I introduce you they won't think that you're some sort of fairy.'

She was closing her front door and locking it. 'You think I look like a fairy?' She tried to sound offended, even though she wasn't.

'It was my first thought.'

Her head cocked to one side. 'And you, Dr James, look like a blond Clark Kent. Do I need to warn everyone that you don't actually wear your underpants over your trousers?'

Olly seemed to take the hint. And the reprimand. 'I'm sorry.'

She perked up and smiled. 'You're so *serious*! I was

joking! I quite like the fact you think I look like a fairy. I'd hate to look boring and normal.'

'What's wrong with boring and normal?'

'It's *boring*. And normal. Be different. Stand out from the crowd. Have a list!' She laughed and he almost looked dismayed at her enjoyment.

'You think I'm wrong to have a list?'

'Not wrong, per se. Everyone has certain requirements for a partner.'

'Exactly.'

'They just don't usually write them down.'

He stopped her from trudging through the snow by grabbing hold of her arm. 'How do you know they're written down?'

She stopped to look at his hand, trying hard not to think of how close it was to her smouldering skin. She met his gaze instead. 'Your father told me.'

'Dad did?'

She nodded and he let go.

They were crunching through the snow now, past Betsy and Olly's car and towards the surgery. It was picture-postcard perfect, with everything blanketed in white.

Lula turned to him. 'You know, Olly, a man like you shouldn't need a list.'

'A man like me? What does *that* mean?'

'A young man. Educated. Good-looking. An eligible bachelor. Though you could do with a different look.'

'What's wrong with my look?'

'Oh, come on, Olly. You think I don't already know that you're considered to be the "hottie" of the village? All the ladies last night at the belly dancing think you're a babe.'

He preened a little. 'Really?'

'Uh-huh.'

'And you?'

'And me what?'

'Do *you* think I'm a babe?'

'Well, as gorgeous as you are, I can tell your look hasn't changed for decades. Side parting…bit conservative. It would surprise me if you didn't have a pair of brown corduroy trousers in your wardrobe. You need to spice yourself up a bit.'

She stopped to look at him, at his dark hair, his bright blue eyes and solid jaw. He was narrow at the waist and broad at the shoulders. He might have been a male model. Olly was the epitome of male good looks, handsome and attractive, and if she was in the market for a man then he'd be the type that she would go for.

But I'm not. And I won't.

'You're okay, though.'

He laughed out loud, plumes of his warm breath freezing in the cold winter air. As she watched him chuckling to himself beside her, she felt a little twinge of regret that she'd sworn off men for good.

Olly wasn't sure what to make of Lula's assessment of his character. He was amused and offended at the same time. What was wrong with having a pair of brown corduroys? They were comfortable and warm and… Oh. Sensible.

Was he *very* sensible? Yes, he was, but he'd always thought of that as a strength. He was a loyal, dependable guy who enjoyed living a quiet life. Better than having to live in a big, noisy city, where no one talked to each other or looked out for their neighbours. Where there was no community spirit.

Lula seemed to think that his life was a little too staid. A little too quiet. Genteel. But when you enjoyed living in a small community it was what you got used to. Lula's arrival in the village, with her rainbow-splashed hair and joyful approach to life, was like dropping a lit firework into a dormant barrel of gunpowder.

She would set off sparks and there would be implications.

Some people might enjoy it. Some people might be glad of it—the village being woken up from its dreamy slumber. *Will I like it?*

He liked *her*. He knew that already. She was bright and funny and clever, and he loved her attitude to life. But he couldn't help but wonder if she would leave him feeling a bit...*beige*. He was so used to a quiet life—answering to no one but himself, really—and he'd resigned himself to the fact that the right woman hadn't come along... He'd always figured he'd end up running the practice when his dad retired. The business would be his. Everyone would expect him to carry on and he'd do it—easily, without complaint...

But what if he couldn't? What if Lula was exactly the sort of person he needed in his life before he lived the entire thing having never done anything challenging or exciting?

He didn't like to think she would make him feel his life was lacking in flavour.

He didn't like to think that she would disapprove of his life.

He wanted to prove her wrong.

It was nice and warm in the surgery. The receptionist made them cups of tea and Olly gave Lula a quick tour. He showed her where her consulting room was, and then they went to his and he instructed her in how to log on to the computer system.

Even though there'd been that morning's drama and they were a little behind, and the waiting room was full, Lula needed to see how to use the practice's system. It wasn't one of the newer ones she was familiar with, but it was quite an easy system.

The home screen for each patient gave a basic rundown of their personal details—name, address, date of birth, current age—and also their current medication, if any, details of their last few appointments and what they'd been diagnosed with. She could take a quick glance at the screen and get a pretty general idea about a patient before they came into the room to tell her their new problem.

Lula sat to one side of Olly and observed as he began to see patients.

First a mother brought her eight-year-old son in. He'd got a tummy ache, and his mother reported that he always got them before school. They had a little chat with the boy who told them that he didn't like school, or the other boys there, and so it was put down to stress and anxiety rather than any sort of bug or infection—or something more dramatic like appendicitis.

Next they saw another mother, much younger this time, with three-month-old twin girls. Basically, she wasn't coping. The twins fed erratically, she'd had to give up on breastfeeding and she felt a failure. They kept crying, and they wouldn't sleep, so neither could she. It was all getting a bit too much.

Olly gave her some information about a twins group over at South Wold, and a short prescription for anti-depressants at a low dosage to see how she got on. He also told her that he would contact her local health visitor and ask her to call in and give her some advice on coping with the babies. She seemed happy with that and off she went, pushing her buggy with the two screaming babies in it. The surgery was much quieter after she left.

Then they saw a woman in her fifties called Eleanor Lomax. Lula sat up straighter when this woman came in, and studied her hard.

Eleanor was fifty-six. On her fiftieth birthday she had found a lump in her breast which had turned out to be cancer. She'd fought the disease and beaten it, but now she was having issues over her health again.

'Every night, Doctor, I lie in my bed and feel a twinge here or there, or a niggle somewhere else, and I keep thinking, *Is this it? Is it back?* I can't sleep for the worry that the cancer will return.'

Eleanor was sitting in her chair very upright, straight-backed and erect. Her hair was already silver, but beautifully cut and styled. She had large brown eyes, shaped like almonds, and a long, thin, aquiline nose in her perfectly made-up face. Her clothes were expensive and she looked like a woman who had refined tastes. Lula could only look at her and wonder...

Olly, meanwhile, was unaware of Lula's assessment and was doing his best to reassure his patient. 'It's perfectly natural to feel this way, Eleanor, after what you've been through. Have you tried talking to your cancer nurse about it?'

'She's so busy. I don't like to bother her.'

'You're not bothering her. It's what she's there for. Have you been to counselling since your recovery? A support group?'

She shook her head. 'That's not my thing.'

'What *is* your thing?' asked Lula.

Olly glanced at her sideways, surprised by her interruption.

Miss Lomax turned to Lula and shrugged. 'I've always taken care of things myself. Supported myself. I don't like to lean on others.'

Lula said nothing more as Olly put Miss Lomax in touch with a support group and gave her a few leaflets about counselling and cognitive behaviour therapy before she went on her way.

When Eleanor had left Olly turned in his chair. 'You okay?'

She nodded. 'Fine.' She didn't want to tell him that she

was wondering if Eleanor Lomax was her mother. The mystery 'EL' she'd been searching for lately.

They saw an old man suffering with diarrhoea, a young man with a sore knee who'd played football with his work colleagues the day before, a baby with a cold, and a woman who'd come in to talk about her daughter.

'She's been very withdrawn lately.'

'And she's how old?'

'Thirteen. It could be puberty starting—I don't know. They get flooded with hormones at this age, don't they? But she's not herself and she hides away in her room all the time and doesn't eat.'

Olly was reluctant to diagnose anyone without actually seeing her. 'Perhaps you could get Ruby to come in? Do you think you could get her here? Then we could weigh her and allay any fears you may have about her eating.'

'I could try, but she's not very cooperative at the moment. Always arguing with us when we do see her.'

'Well, I can't do anything unless I examine her.'

'Could you come out to us?' she asked.

'I only really do home visits if it's impossible for my patients to get to me.'

Lula was surprised by this. She thought that it might be better if Olly *did* try to go and see Ruby at home and she suggested it. Especially after what had happened that morning with the baby. They were looking for a teenage girl. But Olly wasn't too happy about having his methods contradicted, although he tried his best not to show it.

For the rest of the day they saw a standard mix of patients—a lady who wanted a repeat prescription, another lady who had a chest infection and a man who'd come in to discuss his blood test results and was quite anaemic.

A typical day for a GP. Lula even saw some patients of her own.

When the clinic was over, and with only two house visits left to do, they stopped for a cup of tea and a bite to eat.

'Mary might have brought in one of her delicious cakes for us to eat,' Olly said, and smiled.

Mary was the receptionist, and she had indeed brought in a coffee liqueur cake that was rich and moist and devilishly moreish.

'Mary, you *must* give me the recipe!' Lula said.

'I can't do that—it's a family secret!'

'What if I promise not to tell anyone?'

'We'll see, Dr Chance. Perhaps if you stay on then I might give it to you.'

Lula agreed that it was a deal, knowing she would never get the recipe. She had no plans to stay here in Atlee Wold. She was here to do two things. One was to work as a doctor, and the second… Well, Olly was about to find that out.

He sat down in the chair next to hers in the staff lounge. 'Well, how did you enjoy your first clinic here?'

'It was good. Interesting. There's a real community feel to a small village practice that you just don't get in a large city.'

'That's the truth. You can build relationships with people here that go on for years. Not that you can't do that in the city or in towns, but when you live amongst the people you treat, shop in their store, post your mail in their post office, you develop friendships, too.'

'Don't you find it sometimes restricts the amount of privacy you have?' Lula asked.

'Not at all. I don't mind that everyone knows I'm a doctor, and that my father was before me, and that I got the big scar on my leg from falling out of a tree in Mrs Macabee's orchard.'

'Ooh, let's see!'

Lula was always fascinated to see scars and hear the story behind them. She guessed it was part of being a doctor. She had a thing about noticing people's veins, too. Whether or not they had good juicy veins, ripe for a blood test. You developed an odd sense of humour, being a medical professional.

Olly put his tea down and rolled up his right trouser leg to reveal a slightly jagged scar running down the front of his shin. 'Broke my tib and fib. Open fracture.'

'Nasty.' She could imagine the bones sticking out through the skin. The pain, the blood. The panic. She ignored the fact that he had a beautifully muscular leg, covered in fine dark hair.

'Mrs Macabee got my dad and they took me to the A&E over at Petersfield. We were treated by people who were very kind and friendly, but I was just another casualty to come through the door. Here in Atlee Wold we really care about one another.'

'*All* doctors care about their patients, Olly.'

'I know, but you know what I'm trying to say. Don't you?'

She nodded. She did know. She was just playing devil's advocate.

'You say you know a lot about people here in Atlee Wold? Their histories? Does that include everybody in the village? Do you know absolutely *everyone*?'

'Pretty much. Why?'

'Eleanor Lomax. The lady who had breast cancer. What can you tell me about her past?'

'Eleanor? She's a lovely lady. Always lived on her own. Keeps herself to herself. Retired now, but she used to run a boutique, I think. Why?'

Lula shrugged. 'She just caught my attention. Mainly because… Well, to be perfectly honest with you, Olly, I'm not just here to work.' She bit her lip and looked at him to gauge his reaction.

'Or to belly dance?'

She smiled. 'Or to belly dance. I'm here to find someone. Someone whose initials are EL.'

'EL...like your mother? You think Eleanor Lomax might be your *mother*?' He looked incredulous.

'Maybe. I don't know.'

'What makes you think your mother is in Atlee Wold? There must be hundreds, if not thousands of women in the UK with the initials EL.'

'Well, it's complicated...'

'When *isn't* it?'

'When I was abandoned there was obviously some press coverage.'

'Right.' He was listening intently, his brow furrowed.

'The papers asked for my mother to come forward, to let them know she was all right, to see if they could reunite us—that sort of thing. Well, the paper in Portsmouth—the *Portsmouth News*—was sent a letter by someone signing it "EL". The letter explained that she couldn't come forward. That her parents had made her give up the baby, there was no chance of us being together, and that she hoped they would leave her alone.'

'She sounded desperate?'

Lula nodded. 'There was a postmark from the Petersfield sorting office, and the handwriting was very distinctive. A journalist took it around the local post offices, to see if any of the staff could remember franking it, and one did. He also remembered the woman who'd posted it, because she'd been upset and had had red eyes from crying.'

'I can see why he'd remember a crying customer.'

'Anyway, they questioned this man and he said he'd seen her before. Getting off the bus from Atlee Wold.'

'*That's* what you're going on?' he asked incredulously. 'It's tenuous, at best.'

'It's all I have.'

'Did the journalist come here? Try and track her down?'

'He said there were a number of women with the initials EL in Atlee Wold and that none of them would talk to him.'

Olly looked at her. 'Oh, Lula… I wish I had something more constructive to say, but I think you're taking a long shot. It's all hearsay and secondhand, and relying on the memory of a guy who thinks he saw a woman get off a bus once. And EL—whoever she is—could have got off the bus from Atlee Wold to throw people off track.'

'It's better than having nothing at all, Olly. Imagine having that. No idea at all. You're close to your father. You know your family history. You have roots. Just think for a moment how you'd feel if you had none of that. Wouldn't you feel…adrift? A bit lost? Wouldn't a part of you want to know?'

He thought about it for a moment and then nodded. 'I guess so. My mother died when I was very young, so I don't remember her. I've always felt something's been missing.'

'So you understand that I have to try? Because if I didn't then I'd never forgive myself if it turned out my actual birth mother was living within a few miles of me and I never looked for her.'

'And if she *is* here? If you *do* find her?'

Lula smiled. 'Then I'll know where she is. And that will be enough. I'm not silly enough to expect that we'll suddenly fall into each other's arms and have a mother-daughter relationship.'

'And if she rejects you?'

'Then I can't hurt any more then I already do. She already did that once. Remember?'

Olly didn't often find himself not knowing what to say. He was usually the person people went to with their problems and he *always* had some sort of advice to give. But this…this was different. 'I think, Dr Lula Chance, that you are a very brave lady indeed.'

She looked up at him through her purple fringe and her

eyes twinkled with appreciation. 'Thanks, Olly. I appreciate your help.'

'My pleasure. Not that I actually helped much.'

'You listened. And sometimes that's all someone needs.'

'For you, Lula, my ears are always open.'

He passed her another piece of cake and they sat there in companionable silence.

Before afternoon surgery began Olly spoke to his father over the phone.

'So she's looking for her mother? Here in the village?'

'Looks like it.'

'Well! Can't say I blame her…but I can't imagine who it might be.'

Olly nodded, doodling with his pen absentmindedly. 'Neither can I. But I want to help her if I can.'

'You like her, don't you?'

'Dad!' he warned. 'Don't start.'

'I'm not starting,' he replied innocently. 'Just encouraging you.'

'Let me get this straight. You'd *want* to see me with a woman like Lula?' He almost couldn't believe his ears. His father was the most strait-laced man he knew!

'Why not?'

'Well, because she's…'

'She's what?'

Olly wasn't sure how to answer him. 'Out there!'

'She's just what you need. After all that business with Rachel.'

As if he needed reminding. That had been a really dark time. Rachel had barged into his life like a wrecking ball and left just as much devastation behind.

Would Lula do the same?

CHAPTER THREE

AFTER WORK, LULA TOOK herself over to the village library. It wasn't huge. In fact it was barely a library at all—just one small room, lined with books. Since the funding had been cut it was no longer staffed, and it relied on the good-will of its customers to ensure it was looked after and that they signed out their own books.

It was a strange set-up, and for a while Lula felt odd, standing there alone, looking around the small room. One side was fiction, in alphabetical order, and the other side non-fiction, all in the Dewey decimal system. In the cen-tre were racks of children's books and some old DVDs. In one corner, beneath a window, sat an ancient computer and a microfiche reader, alongside a filing cabinet. She headed over.

It didn't take her long to find the electoral roll for the area and, flicking through, she discovered that there were four families with a surname beginning with L in Atlee Wold—the Lomaxes, the Loves, the Lewises and the Lou-thams.

Any of those people might know something about leav-ing a baby on a Portsmouth beach. But they also might know nothing at all. The information she had about EL could be completely wrong. Who knew?

I won't find out unless I investigate.

She looked up and smiled at a little old lady who'd come

in, holding her coat closed against her chest and wheeling a shopping basket behind her.

'Hello, dear.'

'Hi.'

'You're the new doctor, aren't you?'

Lula smiled and nodded. 'How did you know?'

The old lady let out a laboured breath, twinkled her eyes at her and smiled back. 'Can't be many young ladies with a rainbow in their hair. Phoebe Macabee lives next door to me and she told me about your belly-dancing class.'

'You ought to come. It's fun.'

'With my hips? I don't think so, dear.' She rubbed her left arm, absently.

Lula noticed the movement, but said nothing. It didn't have to mean anything, did it? She'd been wheeling her basket—perhaps it just ached? 'It doesn't have to be about the hips, you know. You could still come. Be with the group. Get some shimmying action with the arms?'

The old lady shook her head. 'My shimmying days are over, dear, but thank you for inviting me. You here for a book?'

'Research.'

She looked at the electoral roll in front of Lula. 'You need to know about the people round here?'

Lula shrugged. 'Maybe.'

'Well, I've lived here all my life, dear. I know pretty much everyone. My name's Yvonne, but everyone knows me as Bonnie.'

'Bonnie. That's a lovely name.'

'Thank you.' Bonnie settled into a chair next to her, her bones creaking as she did so, sighing the sigh of a woman who had finally found the time to sit down in the day. 'Now, what do you want to know?'

Lula was unsure of what to say. She appreciated Bonnie's offer, but did she want to tell the old lady *why* she needed knowledge?

Bonnie must have seen the look on her face because the old girl smiled and laid a hand on Lula's knee. 'I can keep a secret.'

'Secrets are the problem. The person I'm looking for has kept a secret for a long time, and I'm not sure I should be allowed to tell it.'

'Are you part of the secret?'

Lula nodded.

'I thought so. Figured you wouldn't be looking, otherwise. Well, my dear, to my way of thinking if you're part of the secret then you can tell whoever you want. I'm discreet, if that helps any, but I know you don't know me from Adam.'

'How about you just tell me what you know about certain people?'

'I can tell you general knowledge. But I can't go telling private stuff. Discreet, remember?'

Lula smiled back. 'Discreet. What do you know about Eleanor Lomax?'

A small radiator affixed to the wall beneath a cork board of notices ensured that the cold outside didn't permeate the small library and Lula and Bonnie sat pleasantly warm, discussing stories and people.

'Eleanor Lomax has had a hard time of it lately,' Bonnie began.

'I know about her health problems.'

Bonnie reached into her wheeled basket for a pile of heavy books and laid them on her lap with a sigh. 'Well, you would, being a doctor. The breast cancer? Yes, terrible it was. I went with her once to the hospital, to sit with her whilst she got her chemotherapy. I tried to stay bright for her, but it's an odd place, the cancer ward. All those people on hiatus, waiting for treatments, waiting for news, waiting to get back to their own lives.'

'It can be difficult.' Lula didn't need telling about that. She'd been there.

'Yes, it can. But she was strong—she fought it and she won. Physically, anyways.'

'What do you know about her before?'

Bonnie tilted her head to one side as she considered her answer. 'She's always lived alone. Never had a man about the place as far as I know.'

'Family?' So far Bonnie hadn't told her anything helpful.

'I think she mentioned a sister once, but there was a bit of a scandal so they don't talk to each other much.'

Lula perked up. A scandal? Like an unplanned pregnancy? That sort of thing could stop family members from getting along. Had Eleanor been forced to give up a baby? Or had she done it willingly and her family hated her for it? Or was it something else entirely and Eleanor Lomax was a woman who had nothing whatsoever to do with Lula at all?

'Does the sister live close by?'

'Over in the next village. She's much older than Eleanor, I think, and not well, last I heard.'

Lula nodded her head. Could be anything. But, as a doctor, she wondered whether she could somehow create a reason for visiting this sister. 'Do you know her name? Where she lives?'

Bonnie looked oddly at her. 'Something important is driving you, isn't it, Doctor? All these questions...'

'Something. Maybe. Do you know?'

Bonnie shook her head. 'No, sorry. But I think her name was Brenda, if that's any help?'

Brenda Lomax. Okay. I can check on that.

Bonnie rubbed at her chest.

'You okay?' There was a slight sheen of sweat on Bonnie's face.

'Touch of indigestion. Now…who else can I help you with?'

'This family…' Lula pointed at the electoral roll. 'The Love family. What do you know about them?'

'There's no "them". There's just Elizabeth.'

Elizabeth. Elizabeth Love. Another EL.

'Yes?'

'Keeps herself to herself. You don't see her much— though she takes in all manner of waifs and strays.'

'People?'

'Animals! Cats, dogs, mice, wildlife… She's got a real animal rescue thing going on up there.'

'Up where?'

'Burner's Road. It's on the very outer edge of Atlee Wold—leads to Burner's Farm. It's quite isolated, but she seems to like that. The vets round here bring her animals to care for and she takes them all in. Prefers them to people.'

Lula listened, thinking about how she'd driven to Burner's Farm just last night. Had she driven past her own mother's house and not known it? How likely a candidate might Elizabeth Love be? Apart from the initials, there weren't any clues.

'What about the Lewis family?'

'Big family. Lots of relatives. Well known around these parts…well liked. Phoebe Macabee used to be a Lewis, until she married her Ron.'

'Any of them have a name beginning with E?'

Bonnie pursed her lips, thinking. 'Let me see… Ron, Davey, Shaun, Marion, the kids… No, I don't think so. Who are you after?'

Lula smiled. 'And the Louthams?' She pointed at their name on the electoral roll. 'Any of *them* have the initial E?'

'Well, there's Edward Loutham…'

She rubbed at her chest again, and now Lula could see

that Bonnie was looking a bit pale and clammy. But if she was ill surely she'd say something?

Since when has someone of Bonnie's generation ever been honest about the extent of their health? She said 'indigestion', but...

Bonnie tried to stand and lift her books to put them on the counter, but she gasped and leant against the unit.

'Bonnie?'

But Bonnie didn't answer. She groaned, clutching her arm, and then she slipped forward.

Lula tried to catch her, to break the old lady's fall, but Bonnie was heavier than she looked and she tumbled to the floor with a thud.

Lula rolled her over. 'Bonnie! Bonnie, can you hear me? Open your eyes!'

No response.

She grabbed Bonnie's shoulders and gave her a small shake. 'Bonnie!' Then she knelt over her, tilting Bonnie's head back and listening and watching for breaths.

She'd stopped breathing.

A million thoughts raced through Lula's head. She needed to start CPR, and she also needed help. She ran to the door of the library and yanked it open. Seeing an old man strolling along opposite, his rolled-up newspaper in his hands, she called out, 'I need help in here!' before dashing back to Bonnie to begin chest compressions.

She pressed down hard, keeping a continuous rhythm, trying to count the beats. She had done the first thirty compressions and was blowing air into Bonnie's lungs by the time the library door opened and the man she'd seen in the street appeared.

'Oh, my goodness!'

'I need you to call an ambulance! And fetch Dr James—see if he's got a defibrillator.'

She had no idea if they did or not. But some remote

areas had them and she could only hope that Atlee Wold was one of them.

After breathing twice for Bonnie, Lula carried on with the compressions. 'Come on, Bonnie.' She pushed and pushed. Up. Down. Up. Down. A continuous rhythm she dared not break.

The library door closed behind her and time went slowly, yet also too fast. To Lula, it seemed as if she was doing compressions and CPR for ages, waiting for Dr James or an ambulance to turn up, when in reality only a few minutes had passed before Olly came rushing in. Thank goodness—he was carrying a small bag.

'Defibrillator?'

He nodded, unzipping the pack and grabbing the scissors to cut open Bonnie's clothes. 'I've called the ambulance.'

She heard him, but couldn't answer. Exhausted, she continued with compressions, her own breath labouring.

Olly looked at her. 'Let me take over.'

They switched places and Lula ripped open the packs that would allow her to attach pads to Bonnie's chest—one on the right side, up near her shoulder, and the second below her left breast. She switched on the machine and heard it give instructions to apply the pads, which she'd already done. She plugged in the cable for the pads and the machine began to assess Bonnie's heart rhythm.

If she was in asystole—essentially a flatline—then they wouldn't be able to shock her. Asystole was a rhythm that couldn't be changed through shocks, and the only thing they'd be able to do would be to continue with CPR until the ambulance arrived. But if she was in ventricular fibrillation—VF—they would be able to shock her and hopefully restart her heart in a normal rhythm.

'Stay clear of patient,' intoned the machine.

Olly stopped compressions and glanced up at Lula, who looked back at him uncertainly, sweating, her hair stuck to her forehead. She noticed tiny things then. Odd things. The snow stuck to Olly's shoes. A small butterfly pin stuck to Bonnie's shopping bag. The way one page of a book near to her, loose and unattached to the spine, stood out over and above all the others.

'Shocking.'

She's in VF!

'Stand clear,' Lula said, checking to make sure neither she nor Olly was touching Bonnie. It would be dangerous for them if they were in contact as she pressed the orange button with the picture of lightning on it.

She shocked Bonnie and waited for the machine's next instruction.

'Continue CPR.'

Olly began again and kept going.

It was hard to think that just moments ago she and Bonnie had been chatting with each other in this little library. Everything had been normal, day-to-day, and suddenly this… *She said she'd had indigestion. I should have paid more attention!*

But her focus had been on getting information about her mother.

Guilt filled her and she bit her lip hard as she watched Olly try to save Bonnie's life.

He stopped to listen for breaths. 'She's breathing!'

Lula let out a breath she hadn't known she'd been holding. *'Yes!'*

'There's oxygen in my car outside. I'll get it.'

Lula put Bonnie into the recovery position whilst she waited for the oxygen and then, when Olly returned, turned on the tank and attached the mask to Bonnie's face. She was breathing well, her breaths steaming up the small mask. They checked her pulse and respirations as they waited for the ambulance, which they could hear in the distance.

'That was quick. I thought they'd be a while.'

'There's a station in South Wold, and a small cottage hospital.'

'That's good.'

'What happened?'

She shrugged. 'We were just talking and she collapsed.'

He looked carefully at her. 'Are you okay?'

She nodded. 'I'm fine.'

The paramedics got Bonnie into the ambulance quickly, attaching her to their ECG machine and establishing a good trace. Lula jumped into the ambulance to go with her to the hospital and Olly said he'd follow later, once he'd finished clinic, to see how everything was and bring Lula home.

Olly and Lula were travelling back in Olly's car. He drove slowly through the snow, but couldn't help but glance at Lula to his left to try and gauge how she was doing. She seemed to be staring, unseeing, out of her window at the snow-covered fields and he wondered if he ought to try and talk. Try and break the silence. He wanted to know if she was all right.

'How are you?'

She turned to him and smiled. Her voice was perky and bright. 'I'm fine.'

His eyes twitched as he questioned her reply. 'Really?'

'Sure.'

'Because it's been a bit of a rollercoaster for you since you came to Atlee Wold.'

'You mean finding an abandoned baby and then having a patient have a heart attack in front of me?'

He glanced back at the road, ensuring he was driving carefully. 'Well, yeah. That'd be enough to freak anyone out.'

'I'm not *anyone*.'

He recalled his first sight of her, shaking her hips. 'I know that.'

'I'm made of stern stuff, Olly.'

He didn't doubt it. 'But finding that baby…having been abandoned yourself. It must have stirred up memories for you?'

'I don't recall the actual abandonment part. I was too young.'

'I know. And then having to do CPR—'

'I *am* a doctor. I haven't always been a GP. I once worked in A&E, and we had to do CPR a lot.'

Okay. A little prickly, maybe. This is one side of Lula I haven't seen yet. But I suppose it's normal, considering her past.

He decided to change the subject. 'So…did you find a good book?'

'I'm sorry?'

'At the library? Did you find a good book?'

'I wasn't after a book. I was looking at the electoral roll.'

He understood then. 'You were looking for your mother?'

'Four families whose surnames start with the letter L. Two of them have people whose names begin with E.'

'Right.'

'Bonnie was telling me about them.'

'Digging for clues, huh?'

'All good doctors dig for clues.'

'Bonnie wasn't in the role of patient at that point?' He steered to avoid a fallen tree branch. 'What did she tell you?'

'She told me about Eleanor Lomax and Elizabeth Love.'

'Elizabeth Love? I'm not sure I know her.'

'She's a recluse, Bonnie says. Runs an animal sanctuary, or something.'

He nodded. He recalled that someone did something like that on the edge of the village, but he hadn't known who. 'And you're going to talk to these ladies?'

'I am.'

'And say what, exactly? If they're not who you think they are don't you think they'll be a bit taken aback?'

'One of them will be taken aback if she *is* who I think she is.'

'You can't go barging in and asking if they're your long-lost mother.'

'Are you telling me what to do, Dr James?'

'I'm advising. And I'm also looking out for my patients.'

'They don't need protecting from me. I'm not scary.'

He smiled. No. She wasn't scary. *Quirky*, yes, but not scary. 'I know. But you know what I'm trying to say.'

'Don't worry, Olly. I won't upset anyone and I'll be very discreet.'

'You have I don't know how many colours in your hair, drive a spotty Beetle, keep rats and spiders, and you'll be *discreet*?' He laughed.

She smiled back at him. 'I *can* be discreet. Just you watch. And it's spider, singular. I don't keep spiders, plural.'

'I do beg your pardon. And you're not worried about people getting hold of some gossip about you?'

'They don't need to gossip about me. They've got you for that.'

'Me?'

'Of course *you*! You've got a list, remember? A list for the perfect wife?'

He felt his cheeks colour.

Ah, yes...that.

'It was a joke, and it was a long time ago.'

'And yet you still don't have a wife? Why *is* that, Olly? You're a professional man, good-looking, you work hard, you have good principles. Why no wife?'

'I don't need a wife to complete me. I'm happy as I am.' He stared straight ahead, his eyes on the road.

She looked at him. 'Even I can tell that's a forced response.'

'I am!'

She sat back in her chair. 'I don't believe you.'

He shrugged. 'That's fine. Though I must say you're the most unconventional person I've ever met, and yet you have such traditional views. Love and marriage? That's nice.'

'You don't believe in love and marriage?'

'I do. My parents had a very strong marriage.'

'So…?'

He quickly glanced at her. 'So what?'

'So why do you seem to go out of your way to avoid it?'

'Is that what I'm doing?'

'You made a list. Of the attributes your perfect wife must have. You're looking for perfection, and perfection is unattainable, so you *know* you're after something that doesn't exist—therefore you're not actually looking.'

'Well, thank you, Sherlock.' He could sense the twinkle in her eyes.

'Because perfection is not out there. *She's* not out there.'

Olly wasn't enjoying this line of questioning. His brow had become a field of ploughed lines and his eyes had darkened. 'I don't think there's anything wrong in having expectations of a future partner.' People needed to know where they stood in a relationship.

'Of course not—if that person has an outside chance of meeting those expectations.'

He glanced across at her. 'You think my list is unrealistic?'

'I do. I think any woman couldn't possibly hope to achieve your high standards.'

'Does that bother you?'

She paused. 'No. But *I'm* not trying to go out with you.'

'Why not?'

Lula laughed in delight. 'What?'

'Why aren't you trying to go out with me?'

She blushed. 'You're a colleague.'

'And you have rules for that sort of thing?'

'Yes.'

'But *I* can't have rules?' Now he was starting to enjoy the banter. Now *he* was on the offensive.

'Your list of the attributes a wife must have is not a list of rules. It's a different thing entirely.'

'So *you* can say you wouldn't date a colleague, but *I* can't say I wouldn't date a colleague?'

Lula bit her lip. Stuck in her own argument.

Olly indicated to turn left and began to head down a smaller lane, with thicker snow. 'You can't be allowed to have a standard, Lula, if I'm not allowed to have one.'

'I'm not saying that. What I mean is… Oh, I don't know what I mean. You've got me tied in knots.' She thought for a moment. 'Saying you'll only date a blonde is not the same as saying you wouldn't date a colleague.'

'Blonde? It's not a list of *physical* attributes. What kind of chauvinistic, shallow man do you take me for?' He was amused.

'So what *is* on your list?'

He let out a big sigh. 'Kindness, dedication, loyalty, a love of family, a desire to have children…'

'Ah, you can strike *me* off the list, then.'

'You don't want a family?' He was surprised. He could imagine Lula with children. She was just the sort to engage young children and he could imagine them being delighted by her, with her crazy hair and fairy-like features.

'I can't have a family, Olly. The chemo…it left me infertile.'

Her voice trailed away and he looked at her and saw her head droop. He'd never seen her look so low. It just wasn't Lula at all. Lula was bright and full of energy—not quiet or sad.

Her answer silenced him for a while. He couldn't imagine never having children. Or being told he couldn't. He hoped they were going to be a big part of his life. Technically, once he had had a child for a little while, even though it hadn't been born.

'I didn't know. I'm sorry.'

'You weren't to know. Besides...you're the first person I've ever told that to.'

He glanced at her quickly—these roads were full of S bends. 'I'm glad you felt you could. I'm really sorry, Lula.'

Olly had counselled people who'd come into his surgery because they couldn't have children, and he'd always had something to say to them. Why couldn't he find the exact right words for Lula? Was it different because she was a colleague?

It has to be. It's not because she's not my type.

'You don't have to apologize. It's not your fault.'

'Still...it's a big part of life that's being denied to you. You must have felt upset when you were told?' He knew how upset he'd been when Rachel had told him what she'd done...

'I was still a child when I found out. It didn't matter much to me then. It didn't seem a big deal.' She shrugged.

'And now?' He really wanted to know.

'And now I can't let it bother me. I fill my life with other things.'

He smiled. 'Rats and spiders?'

'Rats are very intelligent creatures.'

'And spiders?'

She laughed. 'Are more of a challenge.'

Olly turned into Lula's road and pulled up outside Moonrose Cottage. It looked mystical in the moonlight. An old, thatched cottage covered in snow like a frosting of thick icing sugar.

Lula couldn't wait to get inside, switch on the lights and draw up a fire. 'Are you coming in? I could make hot chocolate.'

He thought about it for a minute. He didn't want to impose—she'd barely been in the village five minutes and he felt he'd occupied more than enough of her time already. He was about to turn her down, but there was something about her that he couldn't resist.

'Sounds great—thanks.'

Lula was definitely not the type of woman he would normally go for. All his previous romantic interludes had been with fellow medics who were rather strait-laced and 'normal'. Nothing like Lula. His longest relationship had been with Rachel, and that had been years ago and an utter disaster.

Lula was so far out of 'normal' she was practically an alien from outer space! But he was fascinated by her. By her diminutive size, which made him want to put his arms around her and protect her, and the way the colours in her hair blended so beautifully it was like looking at a mystical rainbow. And those large brown eyes…like pools of chocolate he could dive into…

Calm yourself, Olly! Remember she's not your type!

Inside, he helped her light a fire and soon its crackling warmth filled the small room. They sat before it, enveloping their mugs of hot chocolate with their hands and staring at the leaping flames.

'Eventful day…' he said.

Lula nodded. 'Are all English villages this exciting, do you think?'

'No, I don't think so. It's just got this way since you've arrived. You know, I don't think I've had so many patients visit the surgery, just to see you. You've really brightened up their lives since they did that belly-dancing class of yours, and they can't wait for the next one.'

'I'm glad.' She smiled.

'You're a breath of fresh air.' He coloured as soon as

he'd said it and sipped from his hot chocolate to cover his embarrassment.

Lula glanced at him, nodding at the compliment but wondering if it was the kind of fresh air that *Olly* needed? He needed *something*, the way he was, stuck in his ways.

'Thank you. I try to be.'

He glanced over at her. 'Why do you do it?'

She was confused by his question. 'Do what?'

'Belly dancing? I mean, you're good at it—don't get me wrong—but what made you choose to do it?'

'It was fun, it was different. I thought it suited me.'

Yes, she was definitely different—he had to give her that. For the first time that day he noticed that her delicate fingernails were all painted different colours. Red, pink, pale blue, peppermint-green and lilac. There was even a tiny tattoo on her ring finger of a bat.

A bat!

He smiled to himself and shook his head. She was unbelievable. Normally he would have said that he didn't like to see tattoos on women. He was quite traditional in that sense, and had always associated tattoos with men, but on Lula they were different. She managed to make them look amazing—tiny pieces of artwork, splashes of colour in intriguing places, making him want to know if there were any other tattoos on her body that he couldn't currently see.

Not that he would ask her, he thought, his face flushing again at the thought of slowly peeling away her clothes to reveal a veritable teasing trail of tattoos.

He stood up abruptly, clearing his throat. 'I ought to go. Leave you to your rats and spider.'

'Are you on call?'

'No, Dad's covering tonight.'

'I like your father. He seems a good man.' She looked up at him, her face glowing in the reflection from the warm fire.

Olly nodded. 'He is.' This was better. His father was a safer topic.

'What happened? With your mum? You don't mention her.'

What could he say? That he had no memories of her—only the stories that his father told about the amazing woman that Olly struggled to recall? How it hurt to admit that he didn't remember how it had felt to cuddle her, what she'd sounded like, what she'd smelt like?

He sank back down onto the edge of the sofa. 'She died when I was two.'

'I'm so sorry. I know what it's like not to have a mother. Your real mother, anyway.'

She looked it, too. Truly sorry.

'That's okay. It was a tragic accident. No one could have done anything about it.'

'Do you remember her *at all*?'

He shook his head. 'No. But my father tells me about her, and we've got lots of photos and some family videos. There's one of me and her lying on a picnic blanket, facing each other. She's laughing and smiling and beaming at me with such joy and pride on her face...' The memory of the picture, describing it to Lula, hurt. Olly cleared his throat. 'Dad loved her very much.'

'I'm glad. Though not that you lost her. In a way, I guess it means you had something missing from your childhood, too?'

Olly nodded. Definitely. He'd always been aware that there was a giant mother-shaped hole in his childhood. During his schooldays he'd hated the times when everyone but him had made cards or gifts for Mother's Day. Or when only his father turned up for assemblies or sports days or parents' evenings. When he was still small he'd used to imagine what it must be like to snuggle up to a mother at bedtime. Or to have one stroke his fevered brow when he was sick. To spoil him a bit.

His father had been good at dismissing a lot of his childhood illnesses: *'It's just a cold'* or *'It's just a tummy bug'*. He'd done his best, though, occasionally sitting on the edge of Olly's bed when he was poorly, but it had always been hard for him to switch from 'doctor mode' to 'father mode'.

'I guess so.'

Stuck for something to break the tension, he handed her his mug and thanked her for the hot chocolate.

She walked him to the front door, opened it. He walked out into the snow, his footsteps crunching on its crispy surface. He turned to say goodbye.

'Thank you for your help today, Olly.'

'It was nothing.' He smiled.

'No, I mean it. You've really been so kind about me taking your grandmother's cottage and putting my little zoo in it. I appreciate they must have been a shock.'

He looked deeply into her warm brown eyes. 'I'm learning to expect the unexpected with you, Lula. Don't worry.'

She smiled, then leaned forward to stand on tiptoe and peck him on the cheek.

As her lips brushed against his face he froze, his eyes closing in surprised delight at the feel of her soft, warm lips against his skin. Close up, he could smell her slight perfume, but couldn't identify it. Whatever it was, it was delightful. Summery and warm. A hint of jasmine…?

Quickly he regained control of himself, knowing he probably looked a bit idiotic with his eyes closed, inhaling her scent like a kid on a gravy advert. Flushing, he stepped back further into the snow and wished her goodnight, his heart sinking as she closed the door and he was no longer exposed to the warmth and light of the cottage.

Olly trudged back to his four-wheel drive, his thoughts as deep as the snow.

What was going on?

Am I developing feelings for Lula? I can't be… She's… what? Different? Quirky? No. She's beautiful—that's what she is. Inside and out.

Lula closed the cottage door and touched her lips with her fingers. They were still tingling from the kiss and she was shocked. It had only been meant as a goodnight kiss, a thank-you kiss. It hadn't been meant as anything else.

So why did it *feel* like something else?

I like Olly. He's lovely, yes. But…

She wasn't here to start a relationship.

He can be my friend, but that's got to be all.

It would be too complicated if she allowed a relationship to start up—and with Olly, of all people! He was her colleague. In a small village practice. It couldn't develop into anything. He'd already told her that he wanted to have children, and she couldn't have them, so… No. She couldn't pursue *anything* with Olly.

But he's so delicious!

No, Lula. Behave yourself…

She groaned and took the mugs into the kitchen. She stared out of the window into the white expanse of the still garden. She put the mugs in the sink and saw Anubis in his tank. Sighing, she took a step closer and slowly lifted off the lid.

All I've got to do is put my hand in.

Just reach out.

That's not hard, is it?

But her hands stayed where they were. It was still too scary.

She closed the lid, shivering as Anubis stretched out one long hairy leg and began to move.

'Time for bed, I think.'

Lula switched off the lights and then spent many hours staring at the roof of her bedroom ceiling, lost in thought.

Olly sat at his kitchen table, holding a mug of cold tea and staring into space. Lula had only been here a short while and yet he felt she'd begun to turn his ordered life upside down and inside out.

He felt uncomfortable with it. The last time he'd been thrown upside down with his thoughts had been after Rachel had left. When he'd discovered what she'd done…

Lula isn't anything like Rachel.

Lula's attitude to life was so refreshing. She believed in challenging herself, facing her fears, stepping out of the ruts and taking risks. She followed her heart. But she wasn't whimsical or wishy-washy. She had a purpose, she had fun and she was extremely intelligent.

And he was attracted to her.

Simple as that, really, and that scared him. She was nothing like his perfect woman. Or the vision of a perfect woman he'd stupidly concocted in his infamous list. He'd never expected to be intrigued by a woman with tattoos and multicoloured hair. He'd always thought he'd be the type to fall for a regular woman, with normal hair and her only body decoration being a sedate pair of earrings, perhaps a ring or two. A woman who wore suits to work, who drove a sensible car. A woman with class.

Lula has class.

Was it her differences that intrigued him? Was it the fact that she was so unique and so unlike anyone he'd ever met before that made him unable to help gravitating towards her?

No. It was more than that.

He felt *different* when he was with her. He couldn't explain it. It was as if he was seeing life differently. Through her eyes the world was a place of wonder and possibility again, rather than a world of…what?

Beige. That was what. Lula was right about him. Perhaps he had been stuck in his rut for too long? That thing with Rachel had forced him into it even more. Perhaps he did need his world to be shaken up?

Was Lula the woman to do it?

Did he want her to?

Olly got up and threw his tea down the sink, rinsed out his mug and left it on the drainer, staring into the snow through his kitchen window.

He *did* want her to. But he was worried about letting go of who he was. Would he lose himself? Would he lose the respect of others if he let go and went wild for a bit?

I'm a doctor. A GP. I'm meant to be sensible. People rely on that sensibility.

He'd always been strait-laced. Run of the mill. Down to earth. He'd always thought that was an attractive quality. That people liked to know where they were with him. That he wasn't unpredictable.

But hearing Lula's story—hearing how her life had been, all the challenges she'd faced—had made him look twice at himself.

What challenges had *he* had to face? Just two. The death of his mother and the loss of Rachel and the baby. The one she'd never told him about. And it hadn't been an accidental loss, either…

Even so, regarding his mum, he'd been too young to feel the grief of what the loss of her had actually meant. He'd never known her—not really. He only knew what his dad had told him about her. What a wonderful woman she'd been and how in love with her his dad had been.

And Rachel…? He'd blundered wholeheartedly into a relationship with her, expecting it to be exactly like his father's with his mother. He'd assumed Rachel would be the

same type of woman as his mother. Someone perhaps looking for family the way he was? Dedicated to him.

Only it hadn't happened that way, had it?

Rachel had been so many things, but none of those that
he'd expected. She'd not been as dedicated to him as he'd
hoped, and she'd hated village life. Too rural for her. She'd
been a city girl, through and through, and he should have
seen that from the start.

And then I wrote that damned list! That stupid list!

He'd thought the list would protect him from getting his
heart broken again. That if he only went out with women
whose life goals and attitudes matched those on his list,
then he would be safe from heartbreak and pain and loss.

And what was he doing now? Ignoring the list and falling for the most outrageous, multicoloured, tattooed zoo-
keeper he'd ever met!

Falling for her...

Was he? It felt like it. He knew he couldn't stop thinking
about her. When he was with her he soaked up her vitality
and presence like a sponge, and when she was absent his
mind lingered on her, returning his thoughts to her every
single time, like an obsessed teenager with a crush.

That kiss tonight... Goose pimples shivered over his
skin in torment. The touch of her lips had been magical.
He'd wanted more. Had craved more. And yet...he'd been
afraid to seek it out. What if he pursued her and got it all
wrong? He'd done that before. If he got involved with her,
feeling as he was now, and it didn't work out... Well, he'd
be devastated. Floored. And he didn't need that. He'd had
heartbreak and he didn't want to experience it again.

He sought happiness and love and respect—the type of
relationship his father had had with his mother.

Ideal.

Could he have that with Lula? She couldn't have children, but was that important?

The uncertainty that filled him made his steps heavy as he went up to bed.

CHAPTER FOUR

After a sleepless night, Lula woke feeling exhausted.

She fed Anubis, dropping a couple of crickets into his tank, and then gave Nefertiti and Cleo fresh water. They were pleased to see her, holding onto her fingers with their little pink paws and licking her happily. She loved their ratty kisses and stroked them both before putting them back into their cage. She'd not had them out as often as she'd have liked since moving into the cottage. They were used to free ranging, and she knew she ought to organize some sort of safe play area for them so they could come out more.

However, she'd have to pick her place carefully. This cottage was a rental and she didn't expect to stay in Atlee Wold for long. She didn't want them damaging any of the old furniture in Moonrose Cottage, especially as she knew how much the place meant to Olly.

Olly...

She really liked him. She knew it deep in her soul. They'd just connected so easily, the pair of them. It was easy to be in his company, and it was strange to think that they'd only really known each other for a couple of days. Lula felt as if she'd known him for ages.

He was an old soul in the body of a young, fit, handsome man. But she liked that a lot.

Today Lula was going to be running her own surgery, rather than sitting in with him, and she was looking forward to it. But she was also looking forward to seeing Olly again and finding out if he'd heard anything about the abandoned baby yet. She hoped so. She was worried about the mother. Where was she? *Who* was she? Was she all right? She couldn't imagine what it must feel like to give birth and then abandon the baby somewhere...

Whoever had felt pushed into that situation had to be incredibly scared. Or brave. Or a bit of both of those. Selfless, too. Perhaps whoever it was had hoped that by doing so she would be giving the baby the best chance in life. She'd obviously cared about the baby or she wouldn't have wrapped it up so well, provided it with a hot water bottle to keep it warm in the snow.

Lula slipped her feet into her Union Jack wellingtons and put her pink shoes into her backpack. Wrapping up tightly against the cold, she set off to work.

As she tramped through the snow she waved hello to various villagers who were braving the drifts to get their morning paper and milk from the local store. When she entered the surgery she stamped her feet on the mat, glad to be in the warmth again.

Olly was already there, standing behind the reception desk. He was on the telephone and acknowledged her with a smile. She paused briefly to look at him, slowly taking off her scarf and gloves.

He was very tall and broad. Through his shirt she could see he had some nicely defined muscles, especially in his arms.

I wonder if he works out?

He had a sickeningly flat belly that she would have died for, and a trim waist. Boy, did he look good! Yummy—despite the sensible pale blue shirt and navy chinos. Flushing, she put her scarf and gloves in her backpack and pulled off her wellies to reveal stripy multicoloured socks with individual toes.

'Nice.' Olly pointed at her feet as he came off the phone.

'Thanks. They're cosy. Something urgent?' She was referring to the phone call.

'Just checking on Bonnie and the baby. Both are fine. Baby's taking milk well and Bonnie had a comfortable night.'

'That's great.' She slipped her pink boots on. 'No sign of the baby's mother yet?'

He shook his head, and she could see he was eyeing her boots.

'You ready to heal the sick?'

'As always.' She smiled. 'Though I might just grab a cup of tea first.'

'How's the zoo this morning?'

'They're all well.'

He walked with her into the small staff area, watching whilst she made a cup of tea.

'Want one?'

He nodded. 'Thanks.'

She was aware he was still watching her, and surprisingly she felt quite self-conscious. What had happened?

One tingly kiss and I turn into an awkward teenager again?

'Do you have sugar? I forget.'

'One, please.' He seemed amused by her forgetfulness, but took the drink from her with thanks, their fingers brushing and causing electrifying alertness. She eyed his strong hands wrapped around the mug and wondered what it might be like to be held by them…

Stop it, Lula! You're not here for Olly.

She made an excuse to disappear into her room, switching on the computer and booting up the patient file system. The room was bare of her personality, but it would do for the brief time she was there. Normally she would put her own things up—have her own knick-knacks on the desk to entertain smaller patients and her own artwork on the walls in bright colours to make the room more lively—but she wasn't there permanently. This was just a short-term locum position. She wasn't planning on staying.

Just as soon as she'd tracked down whether her mother was here or not she'd move on. If she did find her mother she wouldn't want to stay in the village and pressure her into anything. She'd keep her distance. And if she *wasn't* here then it didn't matter. She would move on and try… what? There were no other clues. She had to be *here*.

Somewhere.

Her first patient arrived—Arthur Cross. He'd developed a nasty cough, so she listened to his chest and it sounded quite crackly. Concerned about a possible infection, she wrote a prescription for some antibiotics and said good-bye. Next was a young mother with a baby, who wanted to know whether she could go back on the contraceptive pill. Her husband wanted more babies—she didn't. Lula suggested they have a discussion with each other, but wrote a script for it anyway and hoped it wouldn't cause a huge marital argument between the two of them.

She saw a steady influx of patients all morning and was busy. The work kept her mind off her mother, and most definitely off Olly. It was only when it got to about eleven o'clock that she noticed the time, because Olly brought her through another drink.

'Made you a tea.' He put it down on the desk and she took it gratefully.

'Oh, thanks. Busy morning, isn't it?'

'It is. I was wondering if you'd come out with me on a house call later?'

'Oh?'

'Can you remember yesterday we had Ruby's mum in? The teenage girl who was being a bit weird?'

Yes, she remembered.

'Well, the mum's more concerned and has asked us to come out and talk to the girl. If she *is* the mother of the baby left on your doorstep I think I'd quite like some female backup, if that's okay?'

She nodded. 'Sure. You really think it might be her?'

Olly shrugged. 'I don't know Ruby very well. I've only seen her for vaccinations when she was a baby herself. But she's the only possible I've got at the minute.'

'Okay. What time are we going?'

'About two? She's not at school. Refusing to speak or come out of her room for the last day or so.'

Oh, dear. Lula hoped it *was* her, so that they could get her urgent medical attention, but she also didn't want to think that a scared thirteen-year-old had had to go through labour and birth on her own—and then dispose of a baby...

'Get me when you're ready to go. And thanks for the tea.'

He winked as he left and she smiled, finding herself wishing he would come back and talk to her some more.

Oh, my goodness! What am I doing to myself?

Olly could only be a friend. There was no point in having those sorts of feelings or thoughts.

As two o'clock approached Lula hid in her room, eating her lunch and trying to stay out of Olly's way as much as she could. But when he came to collect her she could put it off no longer. She would have to be in the car with him and go on this house call.

But that's fine. It's just a ride out. It's work, not pleasure. There's nothing to be afraid of.

She got in his car, highly aware of how close his hand came to her thighs every time he had to change gear or adjust the heating, but thankfully it wasn't for long. Ruby's family didn't live too far from the surgery.

There was a deep drift of snow beside where Olly parked, so she had to climb out of his side. He held the door open for her as she clambered over the gearstick and proffered his hand for her to steady herself before getting out. Blushing, she took it, hoping he assumed her cheeks were going red from the cold and nothing else. And then they were both tramping through the snow to Ruby's front door.

Olly knocked and they waited.

When Ruby's mum answered the door she invited them in and they went inside, happy to be in the stifling warmth of the house. Lula and Olly removed their snow-caked boots in the hall and padded into the lounge in their socks. They sat down.

'Ruby's still in her room. I told her you were coming but she still won't speak or open the door.'

'Do you want me to go up to talk to her?' Lula offered.

'If you want…but mind the mess. I've not had a chance to tidy up.'

Lula smiled sympathetically, then left Olly to talk to Ruby's mum as she went upstairs. At the top of the stairs were three doors. One had a giant yellow *'Danger! Keep Out!'* sign on it, which she presumed was Ruby's, so she gently knocked and waited for a reply.

'Ruby?'

Silence, except for the gentle murmur of voices coming from downstairs.

'Ruby? It's Dr Chance. Can I come in for a chat?'

Still nothing. It seemed odd. She'd expected something. An outburst. A yell to go away—*something*.

Lula tapped on the door again. 'I'm going to come in.' She took hold of the handle, not sure if it would open or not, and gave the door a push.

It did open.

But Ruby wasn't there. The room was empty.

'Oh, no…'

Lula hurried back down the stairs and into the lounge. 'She's not there.'

Ruby's mum stood up, frowning. 'What do you mean, she's not there? She's got to be!'

'She isn't. The room's empty.'

Ruby's mum hurried upstairs to check for herself and then came back, looking completely bewildered. 'I don't know where she's gone!'

'Does she have any money? Are any clothes missing?' asked Olly. 'Her coat?'

She shook her head. 'I don't know. Let me check.'

She disappeared leaving Olly and Lula in the lounge, looking at each other.

'What do you think?'

'I think she may be our girl,' Lula admitted.

'It's looking like it. Perhaps she did a bunk because she knew doctors coming to the house would notice if she'd just given birth or not.'

Lula glanced over at Ruby's mother as she came back in. 'Her coat's gone, and her boots. She must have sneaked out when I was in the kitchen.'

'Call the police. Give them a description.'

Her mum frowned. 'Why? She's only been gone a few minutes. She's probably at a mate's house, or something.' She noticed the conspiring glances between the two medics. 'Is something going on?'

Lula sat her down. 'A baby was abandoned at my home yesterday morning and we've been trying to find the mother, who we believe may be a teenager.'

'You think Ruby…?' She looked horrified. 'But…I'd have noticed if she was pregnant. She's only thirteen!'

'I know, and it might not be her, but we have to take the possibility into consideration.'

She nodded slowly. 'Right. I'll phone the police, then.'

'Could we check her room? See if there are any signs in there?'

Ruby's mum nodded and picked up the phone. 'Go on up.'

Upstairs, Olly and Lula searched for clues as if they were a pair of detectives. Olly rummaged through Ruby's wardrobe whilst Lula was on her knees, pulling things out from under the bed.

She could see something at the back—a large bedsheet, or something like it—all screwed up into a ball… Grabbing it, she pulled it out and saw that it was covered in blood.

'I'd say this nails it, Olly.'

Olly turned around and his shoulders slumped. 'Poor Ruby. We need to tell the police she's our new mother and it's imperative they find her.'

'She can't have gone far, surely? Perhaps we could organise a search ourselves?'

Olly liked the idea. 'I can get Dad to cover the surgery. We could ask for volunteers to help us search.'

'We need to search the bins, too. See if we can find the placenta—check if it's intact.' If a piece of the afterbirth—the placenta—had been left behind inside Ruby it might cause some very serious complications. Bleeding, haemorrhage or infection.

He nodded. 'I'll do that. Why don't you talk to the police?'

Lula headed downstairs to find Ruby's mother already on the phone with them. She asked to speak to them, too, and informed them of her and Olly's findings. The police responded that they'd send officers straight away.

'We're going to organise a search,' she told Ruby's mother. 'You stay here in case Ruby returns. This is my mobile number.' She handed over a card. 'Call me if she comes back.'

'I want to search, too.'

'We need you here.' She laid a reassuring hand on the woman's arm. 'I know you want to be doing something. But the best place you can be is here. We need to know where to find you if we find Ruby first.'

The solemnity of her words must have hit home, because Ruby's mother nodded quickly and sank onto the sofa.

Olly didn't find anything in the bins, and once the police had arrived at the house they set off to organise a search party.

The village hall was thrumming with locals. A quick ring round the village, asking people to spread the word, had prompted a large turnout.

Lula was touched by how many people from the village had come out of their lovely, warm and cosy homes to go searching in the cold, wet snow for someone who was nothing to do with them—except for belonging to their village.

Most of these people are sixty or over. It's an amazing community spirit...

When Lula had arrived in Atlee Wold she'd been the only person on a search for a mother. Now the majority of the village had turned out to do it.

Not for the same mother, obviously. They didn't know about Lula's circumstances and she wasn't about to share that information—even if it was tempting to ask people what they might know whilst they were all gathered in one place.

No. These people were all here for Ruby. Poor little Ruby, who was probably running scared, unaware that her life might be at risk.

Where is she? It's the middle of winter. It's freezing out here.

Lula couldn't imagine for one second how that poor girl must be feeling. Cold, for sure. Alone, definitely. But what else? What had run through Ruby's head to make her go through labour alone and give up her baby? Like Lula's mother. What was the situation that prompted someone to give up a baby?

It was such a massive thing to do. Once it was done there was no turning back. There would always be that knowledge in your head that you'd given up a baby. Even if the reasons for it had been honourable, even if you'd hoped the child would have a better life somewhere else, there would still be that pain, that hole in your heart, to tell you that something was missing.

Something loved...?

Did my mum love me when she abandoned me? Or didn't she care one way or the other? Has she ever regretted her decision? Does she think about me every day?

Ruby having gone missing was prompting this torment in Lula now. There'd always been some element of it inside her, but she'd always kept it in check before. It had been a fleeting thought, a passing wonder or consideration, soon flattened down by more pressing matters. But here, now, with another abandoned baby and another missing mother, Lula couldn't help but think about her own situation.

Olly stood up behind the table and called the meeting to order. The mass of voices in the room were suddenly silenced as everyone turned to hear what he was about to say.

Lula studied him as he spoke. Tall, straight backed, he'd turned his shirtsleeves back to the elbow and she could see his strong, muscular forearms. He really was an attractive man. Solid, dependable, down to earth. The sort of man you could settle down with.

If that was what you were looking for.

If I was the type to settle down, he'd be the type I'd go for...

She watched the faces of the people from the village. They were listening to Olly's every word, some of them even writing down the description of Ruby as he presented it.

He spoke easily, not afraid of addressing the whole room, and there was a command to his voice that she'd never noticed before. It was reassuring. Even though this was a difficult moment—an awful situation—his voice gave the sense that there was someone in charge who knew what to do. If they all just did as he suggested the matter would soon be settled.

She hoped so. She hoped Ruby would be found quickly.

A police officer then added his bit and Olly sat down, glancing at her with a quick smile.

Lula smiled back, her heart warming. He'd done a great job.

She could only hope that now the village would do a great job and find the poor missing girl.

The police presented a map of the village that they'd segregated into different zones, including the large woods that Olly and Lula had been assigned to. They were all given a whistle to blow if they found Ruby, or any sign of the young teen. With a wish for good luck, the villagers were ready to search, and they stood up with much scraping of chairs and mumbling as they wrapped up in their coats and scarves and headed out into the snow.

Outside, fresh snow was falling. It would almost have been pretty if the situation hadn't been so dire.

Lula got into Olly's car and he drove them to the woods. As he drove Lula glanced at him, seeing the strain on his face, the worry lines across his brow, his white knuckles gripping tight about the steering wheel. She asked him if he was all right?

He glanced at her. 'Yeah, I'm fine. This just reminds me of Mum, that's all.'

'What happened?'

He shook his head. 'Mum and Dad went hiking one year, when I was two. My grandma looked after me whilst they went backpacking in America.' He indicated quickly and took a turning that took them in the direction of the woods they were heading for. 'They were walking the Pacific Crest Trail, but they'd not planned it very well and had picked the wrong time of year. There was a lot of snowfall, but they thought that as they were together they'd be fine.'

'What happened?' she asked, with tenderness in her voice.

'Dad went to get water from a stream and Mum apparently headed out to find some firewood. When he came back to their campsite there was no sight of her, but he wasn't too worried. She was an accomplished walker—he figured she'd be back…not realising she'd slipped on some ice and cracked her head open on a rock.'

'How long did he leave it?'

'Long enough. Thirty minutes? He knew they had a long trek ahead of them that day and thought he'd better track her down. When he found her she was cold and hypothermic.'

'Alive, though?'

He nodded. 'But unconscious. They had no mobile phones then, so he had to go for help on foot. They were miles from civilisation, and by the time he got back…'

Lula swallowed hard, feeling his pain and tragedy. 'She'd died?'

Olly grimaced. 'Dad was inconsolable, apparently.'

'It doesn't mean the same thing will happen today. We could find Ruby quickly. There's lots of people out looking for her.'

'I know. It's just a part of my past that's always haunted me, that's all.'

She looked at him. Was this the reason he never stepped out of his comfort zone? Because he'd seen what could happen if you veered off track?

'It was bound to. If it didn't haunt you then I'd be concerned. It just shows you're human.'

She touched his sleeve in companionable solidarity, glad

that she could be there to comfort him at this time. It was also nice to hear more about him. He knew quite a bit about her, but she'd not really had the time to ask lots of questions about him. Even though it was a dark story she was glad that he'd shared it with her, and it helped her understand him a bit more.

'You like helping people. It's part of being a doctor. It just gets frustrating when you can't help everybody.'

Olly smiled at her. 'Thanks. You're right. That's why I've always enjoyed being a GP. It's grass-roots medicine. Okay, you don't have the thrill of the operating theatre, or CPR, or the exciting stuff most times, but I value its basics and the opportunity it gives me to get to know my patients.'

'Have you ever considered any other type of medicine or did you always want to be a GP? Follow your father into the family practice?'

'I always wanted to be a doctor—I knew that. It was only natural that I became a GP. But did I want to do anything else? No. I don't think so. My heart has always been here.'

The parking area by the woods was empty, and Olly parked the car as close as he could to the stile that marked the entry point. Getting out of his car, Olly walked to the back and pulled out a flask and a thick blanket that he stuffed into a backpack and hoisted over his shoulders.

'Just in case.'

Lula pulled on her gloves and zipped up her coat. It really was cold, and the snowflakes that were falling were large and heavy-looking.

The wood looked mystical in its white carpet, with the icing of snow upon the black, skeletal trees and the crows calling out from the treetops in protest.

It didn't look like the sort of place that might be hiding a teenager. But they needed to look there. They needed to look everywhere.

She almost hesitated to ask. 'Shall we split up?'

'Let's stick together as much as we can.'

'I can't see the path—there's too much snow.'

'Even more reason to stick together. If we wander off track it could become hazardous. There's a stream somewhere in there, and lots of dips and hidden rabbit holes. There's even a badger sett.'

Lula nodded, hoping neither of them would get an injury searching through what might be hazardous terrain. They could easily drop through a snowdrift and twist an ankle in a rabbit hole or something.

'It's a pity we haven't got a sniffer dog.'

'If we don't find her that might be the next stage for the police.' He looked grim.

They put their whistles around their necks and clambered over the stile.

Their search for Ruby had begun.

CHAPTER FIVE

'RUBY? *RUBY!*' LULA called out loudly, but the vast emptiness of the woods and the thick layer of snow seemed to steal her voice away.

Everywhere was pure white, and it was hard work walking through the deep drifts, lifting their knees up high for each step. It was like a winter workout. A workout that had both of them huffing and puffing within minutes.

The ground underfoot seemed not only slippery but uneven, and full of unseen hazards. Occasionally Lula spotted a perky-looking robin, hopping here and there, searching for food, but mostly she just saw the crows up high and hoped they weren't an ominous omen.

There were a few animal tracks, but from what she wasn't sure. She scanned the ground, hoping to see a trail of footprints, but if there had been any they'd already been covered by the thick falling snow.

Olly's thick blond hair was covered in snowflakes and his cheeks were rosy. Looking at him, it was easy for her to imagine that they might have been on a pleasant winter walk, but the frown lines around his eyes and across his brow spoke deeply of his determination.

'Ruby?' he called.

There was no response.

They tramped on through the snow, hoping they were

sticking to the path. At one point Lula stumbled, and she reached out automatically for him.

'Are you okay?' he asked, concern in his voice.

'I'm fine! Just a tree root or something…' She was anxious to reassure him, aware of how worried he might be.

But he pursed his lips and took her hand, slipping his fingers through her gloved ones. 'Let's take no chances.'

Lula's cheeks warmed at the contact and for a moment she didn't say anything. It felt strange to be walking through the woods holding Olly's hand. When had she last walked anywhere holding *anyone's* hand?

Years—that's how long. But this is nice…

His hand was strong and firm. His grip relentless. There was definitely no way he was going to let go of her and let her stumble again. Though he didn't seem affected by the contact the way she was.

Perhaps he's just much better at hiding things than I am? I've always worn my heart on my sleeve.

Or perhaps he was just keeping his mind on their task?

It might have amused her to know that his heart was actually racing. When she'd stumbled his stomach had flipped and his heart had almost literally gone into his mouth. He'd offered his hand without thinking. But now that he was holding her tightly he was intensely aware of the contact he had with her. He was doing his utmost to try and keep his mind on the task and definitely *off* the image in his head of pulling her into his arms and kissing her in the snow.

That would be kind of romantic. Kissing her whilst snowflakes fall gently onto our faces…

Lula felt him shiver and saw him mentally shake himself. She wondered if he was reliving that story about his mother. Wanting to offer her support, she gave his fingers a little squeeze and noticed him glance at her.

'We'll find her.'

He nodded. 'Let's hope so.'

'She must be freezing if she's out in this.'

'Let's just hope she's conscious.'

Yes, Ruby would need enough medical attention already, having recently given birth, but if hypothermia had set in as well… A lot of people thought hypothermia simply meant you'd got a bit cold and needed some hot soup and a quilt wrapped round you, but it could be so much more life-threatening than that.

If you had hypothermia your body was unable to produce the range of protective reflex actions it would normally when you were cold. For example shivering—the activation of a mass amount of small muscle contractions—would be totally absent eventually, although at the onset of hypothermia shivering could be quite violent. People could become delirious, and also struggle to breathe or move about. They could suffer loss of judgement and reasoning and therefore end up in further dangerous situations.

What if Ruby had got herself into difficulties? What if she was already bleeding heavily and suffering hypothermia, too?

Lula trudged on, her head down, holding tightly onto Olly. She was glad she was out here with him. He seemed so dependable. So reliable. She knew he was the type of man you could trust.

The type of man you could love?

She glanced at him. Yes, he was. Easily. And that was why he needed to remain her friend and nothing more. She could imagine, in another situation, falling for Olly easily—but she wasn't here in Atlee Wold for that. She wasn't living her life to fall for anyone. There wasn't much point. There was so much else she had to do in her life—fitting in all the things she wanted to do.

Since the leukaemia and the diagnosis of her infertility Lula had made a vow to herself to live life for *her*. Experience everything. Do anything. She couldn't get bogged down in a relationship. She didn't want to have to ask anyone's permission to do anything. She wanted time and space to be her own person. Olly could still be a good friend. There was nothing wrong with that. But that was all she could offer him.

Friendship.

She knew that people were capable of having relationships even though they knew they couldn't have children, but Lula believed the need to procreate was strong in everyone. If you got into a relationship with someone the desire to have a child with them would be a natural progression. She didn't ever want to be the cause of heartache and pain to someone else.

She knew what that felt like already.

She'd tried it.

There'd been a boyfriend during medical school. Gavin. He'd been carefree and happy and fun, and they'd gone out with each other knowing that fun was all they could have together. She'd told him about being infertile and he'd said he was fine with it, that he didn't need to have children, that he had her and that was all that mattered.

Only it wasn't.

Gavin had eventually changed his mind. Said he wanted children in his future. It had caused many arguments and heartbreak, and when they'd split up Lula had vowed never to get into a serious relationship ever again.

And she hadn't.

And I can't now, either.

Olly wanted a 'perfect' wife. Someone kind, considerate and loving—and someone who wanted to have children. He'd said it himself that time, driving home from the hospital. As far as Lula was concerned Olly had a big red cross painted over him, marking him out as unavailable.

Olly wanted children in his future. His traditional future. He was a traditional guy, after all. And she could picture him at some rosy point in that future with a wife and little sandy-haired children running around.

Lula couldn't give that to him. Not in a million years.

Yes, there was adoption, and fostering, and all of that was great, but the need for your own biological child could still be a strong one. Knowing she could never provide a man with that was a big reason for her to stay away.

Because I don't want to get hurt, either.

What would be the point in investing all that time in a relationship? Of loving someone only to have to break your own heart when it all fell apart at the end? Because it always did in Lula's world. Children's homes…foster parents…Gavin. It all broke down when someone wanted something more than you could give them.

'Ruby?' she called out.

Her voice echoed out in the white emptiness. They needed to find the teenager—and quickly. Hopefully she was at a friend's house, or something as safe and un-terrifying as that. Hopefully this search wasn't actually necessary. Perhaps she'd hopped on a bus and gone into town? Did Ruby have a mobile phone? She'd not asked the mother. If she did, she presumed someone would have called it by now.

Lula had to assume Ruby didn't have a phone, or that she wasn't answering it. It would be nice to think that Ruby was tucked up somewhere, warm and safe…

'Ruby? Are you out here?' she called again.

Nothing.

Silence.

Just the crows up above.

How had it felt for Ruby to place her baby on Lula's doorstep and walk away? How had it felt for her own mother to place her on that beach and then leave? What did that do to a person? They had to be distraught. Heartbroken. Not thinking clearly.

They tramped on, Lula clutching Olly's hand, each hearing the other breathing hard, feeling the other stumble or slip occasionally, holding on tightly, not wanting to let go.

It had been a long time since Lula had truly felt a part of a team. She'd always kept herself on the sidelines. Involved, but not *part* of things.

But here in Atlee Wold, with Olly, she could feel just how easy it would be to accept the place and him into her heart. It felt so right. It felt so...

Tempting!

But I can't. It wouldn't be right. Olly wants so much more from a woman...

Strangely, she felt tears prick at her eyes and quickly blinked them away. Where had that emotion come from?

I can't cry!

Lula needed to keep this light-hearted. A fun, surface emotion—nothing too deep. When had she last cried?

I can't remember.

She had once believed that a woman was entitled to a good cry every month. But Lula hadn't cried for a long time. Why was that?

Perhaps not allowing myself to truly connect with people has done that?

With her spare hand she wiped the tears away with her glove and hoped Olly thought her eyes were watering from the cold. She could feel her nose turning red. Looking at Olly, she could see that his had turned a rosy colour, too, as they both huffed frozen breaths out into the air. She wanted to sniff—her nose was running...

Suddenly Lula slipped. Her left ankle went sideways, her foot caught some ice and she fell down, crashing onto her knees.

'Oof!'

The ground beneath was solid and icy and the snow soaked her trousers.

'Whoa! You all right?'

Olly knelt down beside her, his hands on her upper arms, care and concern in his bright blue eyes. The plumes of his frozen breath encircled her face and she tried hard not to stare into his eyes.

'Yes, I'm fine.' She thanked him and got to her feet, tenderly testing her ankle.

'I told you it was dangerous. Perhaps we've gone off the path a bit?'

Olly looked around them and thought that maybe they *had* veered off track. The natural track through the trees was off to the right.

'Come on—hold tight.' He grabbed her hand again and they continued to walk, though her ankle felt a little delicate. She knew she hadn't twisted or sprained it—the pain wasn't bad enough for that—but she'd certainly jarred it.

The ability to see the surface you were walking on was something everyone took for granted. But when that view was obscured—when you didn't know what you were walking on, or walking through—you couldn't have any idea of how dangerous it was. You had to trust to luck…or trust the person who walked alongside you.

I trust Olly. I know he's a man I can trust.

She knew she had to stop thinking of him in that way. But she couldn't help it. He was just so easy to like and depend upon, and those good looks of his didn't help any. He had a natural wholehearted appeal. He was a handsome, kind-hearted and generous man, who happened to be single, who happened to be holding her hand and trying to protect her. What was there not to like?

It would be so easy to kiss him and get carried away.

Even though her cheeks were already rosy from the cold and the exertion she flushed a deeper colour and felt her heart skip along a whole lot more merrily than it already had been! Thinking of Olly in such a way made her stomach do a tiny flip, too. It was like having a whole heap of cheerleaders in there, egging her on to find out how it would truly feel if she did give in to her desires and grab Olly and kiss him.

'Ruby?' she called again, trying to take her mind off her train of thought.

The track ahead curved off to the left, and then it looked as if there was a natural fork in the trail. She felt Olly slow, and when they got to the fork he stopped and frowned.

'The path splits. We need to check both ways, but I'm not happy about you going off on your own.'

'I'm sure I'll be fine. I'm a grown woman. I've looked after myself this long without getting hurt.' She smiled to take away some of the harshness of her words. She didn't want to offend him.

'But you've already slipped once, and you don't know these woods.'

'Do you?'

'A little—though I must admit I've never had the opportunity to enjoy them fully during the summer. Always too much work on.'

'Well, we need to check both paths if we're to search properly. Do the paths conjoin further on?'

'I think so. I'm sure I can remember Dad telling me they did. But it's been so long…'

'I'll be careful, Olly.' She pulled her hand free from his tight grip. 'You be careful, too.' She could see the uncertainty in his eyes.

'Blow your whistle if you see any sign of her or get into trouble.'

'I will.'

'Promise me?'

If someone could market the perfect picture of a face filled with concern, then Olly was it. It was nice that he was so worried about her. But Lula was used to looking out for herself.

'I promise.'

As she set off down her path she realised she could no longer feel her toes or her fingers. The socks she was wearing were normal socks, not hiking socks. They weren't fit for the purpose of trudging through deep snow for hours.

I wished I'd thought of that earlier.

She held on to the whistle around her neck as she hiked through the thicker snow. Looking over, she could see that Olly was now out of sight. Perhaps he'd gone down a dip, or the number of trees was blocking the view of him. It felt good to know that he was somewhat close, though.

'Ruby?' she called, hearing Olly call the same thing in the distance.

There were indentations in the snow, so it looked as if someone might have walked this path earlier. She had no idea if it had been Ruby. It might have just been a dog walker.

'Ruby? It's Dr Chance!'

No response still.

She trudged on, slipping slightly, feeling the ice beneath the surface snow. As she went to correct her balance, putting all her weight on her left foot, the snow gave way. She landed with a thump on her coccyx before sliding part way down a bank and into icy-cold water up to her bottom.

'Oh!'

When she struggled to a standing position the water was only ankle-deep, but her boots were going to be ruined and the back of her trousers was cold and soaked. The base of her spine hurt where she'd fallen directly on to it and she felt slightly winded. Turning, she noted the muddy track of her slide down into the water.

'Great. Just what I needed.'

There was no way to tell where the edge of the small

stream was, so she lifted up her feet in her water-filled boots and tried to find the bank. A tree root stuck out slightly, so she reached to grab for that and pulled herself through the water and up onto firmer ground.

Her feet and legs were *freezing*!

Normally Lula loved snow. Loved the excitement of it and the fun of it. But having soaking wet, freezing cold feet in soggy socks and boots wasn't much fun. She wiped the mud off her bottom and clambered up. At the top of the bank she pulled off one boot and poured out the water. Then she did the same with the other foot. It felt awful to have to slide her feet back into them when all she could think of was warm, cosy slippers, or dry feet wriggling in front of a roaring open fire.

But she did it. She had to.

She continued on, cursing every step, feeling the ache in her bottom gradually fade away.

By the time she met up with Olly again a good twenty minutes had passed and her teeth were chattering.

'Any j-j-joy?'

Olly looked her up and down. 'You're soaked!'

'N-Not really. I'm more ice now than water.' She managed a smile.

'You can't go on like that. Come on—I'll take you home.'

'We need to look for Ruby.'

'And have my new doctor get hypothermia? I don't think so.'

'But the police think we're looking in this area. We can't leave.'

'I'll let them know what's happened and how far we searched. First rule of emergency support: make sure it's safe for yourself. I won't have you walking around in those boots and wet trousers.'

'What if I refuse?'

He looked hard at her, his steely blue eyes firm and sure.

But then a hint of a twinkle filled them before he scooped her up into his arms suddenly, the way a groom might carry a new bride over the threshold. 'Then I'm forced to do this.' He looked into her eyes with amusement, daring her to say anything.

Lula blushed, but also laughed. Olly was strong. She could feel him holding her tightly and safely in his arms. 'Why, Dr James!'

He grinned and began walking the path back to the car. 'Let's just hope I don't hit the ice or we'll both be doomed.'

Lula didn't think he'd continue to carry her all the way back to the car. It was so *far*! But somehow he did. Okay, he was huffing and puffing, and his cheeks were fiery red, and she'd sagged slightly in his arms by the time they got there, but he still held her. He only put her down when they reached the stile at the entry point to the woods.

'Thank you. You didn't have to carry me so far.'

'Yes, I did. I couldn't have your feet in the snow. Not wet like that.'

'Well, it was very chivalrous of you.'

He accepted her thanks with a grin and a nod of his head. 'I do try to be a gentleman.'

'You do it very well. This maiden is thankful.'

She smiled then, and kissed his cheek, but when she pulled away her smile faltered as she saw the way he was looking at her mouth. As if he was hungry for her. As if he was going to kiss her back and it wasn't going to be a friendly peck.

Hurriedly, suddenly afraid of what she might do if she let him, she turned away and clambered over the stile, her whistle clinking against the buttons on her coat. Lula waited on her side of the car, glad that she had the space of a car between them, but clambered in eagerly when he opened up her side and turned on the heater.

Hot air billowed into the car and gratefully she peeled

off her boots and socks and perched her bare feet up on the console, near one of the heating vents.

'Oh...*bliss!*'

Her toes were very pale—almost white. She wriggled her toes to try and feel them, to try and get some life back into them, whilst Olly reversed out of the car park.

They passed some other searchers on the way back, identified by the whistles on their lanyards.

When they got back to Moonrose Cottage Olly insisted on carrying her to her front door.

'I can walk!'

'In bare feet?'

He scooped her out of her seat and once again carried her easily up to the front door. She had her keys ready and unlocked the door. She waited for him to set her down.

'I'll restart the fire.'

He nodded. 'I'll make you a hot drink.'

She watched him disappear into the kitchen. She scooped a pair of thick boot socks off the back of a chair and was just stacking some bigger logs onto the burgeoning flames when she heard him call out.

'Lula?'

'Yes?'

'Have you been in the garden shed?'

There was a garden shed?

'No, I haven't.'

'The door's hanging open. There's tracks.'

Lula padded into the kitchen, her brow lined in question.

But Olly had already unlocked the side door and set off into the garden. From the window, she watched him traverse the long length of the garden towards a ramshackle old shed that she'd not noticed earlier. Then she saw him dash in and heard him calling her name.

Lula rushed to the back door, unable to go out since she

had nothing on her feet but clutching the door frame, hoping he'd found Ruby.

He had.

Moments later Olly emerged sideways from the shed with a pale young girl in his arms, wrapped in blankets. He carried her all the way up the garden.

Two maidens in one day.

'Be careful! It's slippery!' Lula warned. She didn't need him to fall over now and drop the young teenager in the snow.

He carried her into the house and Lula rushed to the front room to pull one of the chairs in front of the now roaring fire.

'I'll make her a hot drink.'

Normally Lula wouldn't give someone needing medical attention any drink or food, in case they needed an operation, but with Ruby it was essential she be warmed up slowly. As neither of them had any warm intravenous fluids handy to push into her veins, blankets, a fire and a hot drink would have to do.

When she hurried back into the front room, holding a steaming mug of sweet tea, Olly was just getting off the phone.

'I've called for an ambulance.'

'Notify the police, too. Call off the search.'

He nodded and flipped open his phone once again.

Lula knelt in front of the young girl, noting her pale features, the way she clutched the blankets. She was still shivering—which was good. It meant true hypothermia hadn't set in.

'Sip this. Slowly.' She held the mug to Ruby's lips and waited for her to take a sip. The solitary action seemed to exhaust the young girl. 'Oh, Ruby! Everyone's been looking for you. Your mother's been frantic.'

'E-E-Everyone?' she stammered.

Lula nodded slowly. 'A lot of the village came out in an organised search. And the police…Dr James and I.'

'I d-didn't know where else to go.'

Lula offered the tea again and Olly returned to kneel by her side. 'The police are on their way.'

Ruby looked frightened.

'It's okay, Ruby. They just want to make sure you're all right.'

'Am I in t-trouble?'

They both shook their heads, though truthfully neither of them knew exactly how Ruby's mother might react. Would she be angry that her daughter had disappeared and had a baby in secret? Or would she cry? Ask questions? Be sympathetic? Understanding?

'You had a baby, didn't you?' Lula asked.

Ruby met her gaze and tears welled up in her eyes. 'It hurt.'

Lula and Olly smiled. 'Of course it did. You were so brave to go through it on your own. Where did it happen?'

'In my bedroom. Mum was at work, so no one heard.'

'We searched the house. Didn't find any sign of the afterbirth or anything.'

'I used a plastic sheet. Mum p-painted the hall a few weeks ago, in time for Christmas, and bought plastic sheets to protect the carpet. I used one of those.'

'Where did you dispose of it?'

'The public litter bin by the church.' She sipped at the tea a bit more. 'That's good.' She paused briefly, her eyes welling once again, before she asked, 'How's my baby?'

Lula patted her knee. 'Good. Safe and warm in hospital. You did a good job, wrapping her up warm and placing that hot water bottle under her. It kept her safe. Though you were lucky I found her. I'd only just moved in. Did you know that?'

Ruby nodded, pulling the blankets tighter around her.

'When I was smaller I used to play here in Mrs James's garden all the time. She used to let me play in the orchard at the bottom, and the shed was my Wendy house of sorts. She put an old chair in there, an oil heater, and some blankets for when the weather was cold and I didn't want to go home.'

'Why didn't you want to go home?'

'My mum and I didn't get along and Mrs James was always kind. Like a grandmother to me.'

'You knew my grandmother?' Olly asked.

'Very well.' Ruby smiled. 'She was lovely. When I'd left the baby on the doorstep I was so tired, and it hurt to walk, I knew I had to rest and I remembered the shed. I hoped the heater still had oil in it and it did.'

Lula looked incredulous. 'You were in there all that time?'

Ruby nodded.

'I never noticed. How did I not notice?'

'There weren't any lights. How would you know?'

She looked at the young girl. 'You could have frozen to death.'

'I was too tired to care.'

Lula glanced at Olly, trying her best not to cry at the young girl's revelation. He reached out and rubbed her shoulder in support.

She blinked away the tears. 'We were worried that you might have a retained placenta.'

'What's that?'

'It's where not all of the afterbirth comes away.'

'It seemed okay.'

'Are you in pain now?'

'A bit. But isn't that normal after giving birth?'

They all heard a siren in the distance, getting closer.

'I'm in so much trouble!' She began to cry.

Lula knelt forward and wrapped her arms around the

young girl. She still felt so cold! And she was shuddering and shaking from crying so much.

It broke her heart to think of what this young girl had gone through. Had her own mother experienced the same thing? Had she been through labour and birth alone and then left Lula on the beach because she'd been too scared to tell anyone she'd had a baby?

As the ambulance stopped in front of the property and Olly let the paramedics in Lula vowed to stay by Ruby's side until the young girl's mother arrived.

Why should she be alone ever again?

Why should either of them?

Olly followed the ambulance to the hospital. Stuck in his own vehicle, he keenly felt his separation from Lula. She'd connected to Ruby—he could see that. She was obviously viewing her own past and abandonment in light of what had occurred with the young teenager.

He felt good that they'd found Ruby and that this story might end well. He hoped so. He could only hope that Lula would find her happy ending, too.

I'm going to help her find her mother.

It was the most important thing to her. How could he *not* help? And if Lula found her mother within Atlee Wold then perhaps she'd stay. There'd be no reason for her to leave, would there? And if she stayed, that meant…he could have a future with Lula in it.

Parking his vehicle in the car park, he strolled into A&E, waving at one of the receptionists he knew. Sally beckoned him over.

'Dr James! Good to see you. How long has it been?'

He was keen to get to Lula and Ruby, but he didn't want to be rude. 'Too long, Sally. How's Jack?' Jack was Sally's husband—a stroke nurse.

'Good, thanks. Getting all nervous about his parachute jump in May.'

Parachute jump? Was the whole world going mad and doing crazy things? 'Parachute jump?'

'It's for charity. They're raising money for brain tumour research. You could do it, too!'

Sally passed him a fundraising form and he took it, doubt in his head. But then he thought of Lula, and what she'd do and say if she knew he'd turned down an opportunity like this.

But did he want to throw himself out of an aeroplane to prove that he wasn't stuck in a rut? That he did occasionally challenge himself? Heights didn't bother him—but then he was normally inside tall buildings or planes, not about to throw himself out of one...

'I don't know...'

Sally smiled. 'It's a good cause. Think how you'll feel when your feet touch the ground.'

His feet *always* touched the ground. He liked them there. It was safe.

But wasn't that the issue?

Olly stared at the form.

Then at Sally.

He nodded.

CHAPTER SIX

IT WAS A LONG wait at the hospital. For the second time in two days, Lula sat by a patient's bedside, watching her sleep.

Ruby's mother had arrived—frantic, weeping, shaking with relief—and she and the young girl had had a tearful reunion. Ruby was physically all right, thankfully. No retained placenta, normal blood loss and she'd been slowly warmed up. Then the nurses had asked if Ruby had wanted to see her baby.

Ruby hadn't known how to answer, but her mother had answered for her. Yes, they wanted to see the baby—because Ruby's mother wanted to know if they could bring her grandchild home.

That had made Lula cry. It might have been a tragic story, Ruby and her baby. It might have had a disastrous ending. But it hadn't. The family was being reunited. As Lula had hoped all along. It hadn't happened in time for *her*. No one had found or tracked down EL from Atlee Wold for *her*. There'd been no desperate search in the snow for *her*.

Lula had remained alone. And then ill and alone. Until the Chance family had come along and offered her home comforts and love. She'd been grateful to them, but she had always known she didn't belong. That she wasn't one of them. That it wasn't her real family. And that yearning for actual roots, for actual blood relations, had burned her deep inside.

Olly hadn't had a mother, either. Was that why he was looking for perfection? Was that why he kept everything safe and normal? So that he didn't have to feel different from everyone else?

Because that was how not having a mother had felt to Lula.

Being on the outside, always looking in, had given her a tendency to keep away from people. When had she ever got involved with anyone? Deeply enough for it to hurt when it was over?

Just once.

But there was something different about being in Atlee Wold. The people, the community feeling... It was hard to describe, but Lula felt at home here. As if she was in the right place. She *knew* her mother was here. Maybe even her father? Who knew? And the urge to stay was strong, even though she knew the chances that her mother wouldn't welcome her with open arms could be strong. What if her mother wouldn't acknowledge her? Wanted nothing to do with her?

Well, that would hurt, but I'd cope with it.

Lula knew that if she was to stay strong then no matter how the search ended she'd have to walk away. Give her mother space. Give herself space and time to reflect. She'd have to put miles between them so as not to come on too strong and demand more from her mother than her mother was able to give. To build their relationship slowly if there was a chance of one.

Perhaps her mother had yearned for her over the years? It was possible, wasn't it?

I do hope so.

And the chance to learn about the choices her mother had made would give Lula some closure, too. Nobody wanted to feel not wanted. Not loved. Especially by their parents. It was meant to be an unbreakable bond, the bond between a mother and her child.

Just to know that she held me in her arms and loved me...

Lula wanted that feeling very much.

Olly drove Lula back from the hospital once again, glancing over at her, looking at her secretly, hoping she wasn't noticing how much he looked at her. It wasn't like her to be this quiet. In the short time he'd known her she'd always been so bubbly, always so full of something to say. It was strange to have her so quiet.

He knew the situation with Ruby must have hit home with her. He knew she was searching for her mother and he hoped she would find her. But he had no real idea of the anguish she was in.

He could only imagine it.

It must be terrible and he wanted to comfort her. Make her better. He decided to take the plunge and dive straight in.

'Guess what I'm going to do?'

He felt her turn to look at him. 'What?'

'You won't believe it.'

'Try me.'

He grinned, his stomach flipping over in shock as he finally admitted to it out loud. 'A sponsored parachute jump.'

Now she was *really* looking at him. *'What?'*

He could hear the delight in her voice, the surprise and the joy. It thrilled him immensely—much more than he'd expected it to. Pleasing her made him feel good. Made him acknowledge that he'd stepped out of Mediocre Land and was going to take a huge leap into Extraordinaryville.

'Really.'

'That's great, Olly! And so brave. I'm not sure I could do it—I'm afraid of heights.'

'I'm sure you'll think of something to challenge it.'

Back at Moonrose Cottage, she invited him in and he nodded his head, wanting to make sure she was okay before he left for the night. It was late. Almost eleven.

The fire had died out and there was a slight chill to the cottage, so he reset the fire whilst Lula sat on the sofa, holding an old quilt around her.

She looked so sad. It was an emotion he didn't associate with her and he so wanted to put it right. There was something about Lula that reached out to him and made him care. Something he'd never experienced before.

The flames took hold slowly, building into a strong red-orange heat. As the wood spat and crackled he sat back and took a seat beside her, taking her hand in his, squeezing her fingers.

'Will you be all right?'

She smiled and nodded at him. 'Sure. It's just been an eventful couple of days, that's all.'

'You can say that again.'

The flames were reflected in her eyes, dancing and leaping, and he suddenly found himself fighting the urge to reach out and stroke her face. Her skin looked so soft in the firelight. Instead he clenched his hands together, as if they were still cold, to stop himself from reaching out.

'I mean, this must have touched you...personally?'

Lula smiled again, and nodded, and he could see tears glazing her eyes. His stomach ached at the thought of her hurting, and as a solitary tear ran down her rosy cheek he couldn't stop himself. He had to reach out and wipe it away.

She looked at him as he did so, her eyes full of something he couldn't decipher. He was too busy trying to understand the feelings ripping through his own body with the force of a blizzard. Only it wasn't cold. It was intense heat. Heat he'd not felt for a long time.

'I can't help but think that…'

She didn't finish her sentence. She just looked at him, and he saw her gaze drop to his mouth, then move back up to his eyes again.

Should he kiss her?

She was his colleague. The new doctor. A locum. A drifter. She wasn't the type of woman he would normally go for. Lula was…*different*. And not just because she had the colours of the rainbow in her hair and a jewel in her belly button and tattoos on her toe-ringed feet. It was none of that. That was all window dressing.

It was Lula herself. So full of life! So full of spark! Always concerned for others, reaching out, doing that little extra. Never asking for anything herself even though she had her own troubles, her own concerns, her own needs.

She was funny and beautiful and kind and caring, and she made him feel he could achieve anything he wanted to. She made him feel as if…he wanted to kiss her.

Olly leaned in. Slowly.

What if she rejects me? What if…?

He never finished the thought because his lips touched hers and an explosion went off in his gut. His eyes closed as he sank into the kiss with Lula, enjoying the soft, sensual curve of her lips, the warmth of her mouth, the scent of her skin.

She didn't protest. She didn't push him away.

She welcomed him!

He took hold of her face and pulled her close, deepening the kiss.

She moaned a little and he couldn't help himself. He lost control at the sound. He pulled her to him, pressing her small, lithe body against his as his tongue delved into her mouth to claim her, taste her, enjoy her.

Lula was something else. He'd never, ever experienced this sort of passion with a woman before. Yes, there'd been heat—but it had been perfunctory and fleeting. A case of him just going through the motions.

But this… This was something else!

'Olly…' she breathed as his mouth left hers to cover her jawline and sink down her throat, nibbling her skin and kissing, biting and licking at her pulse points. She smelt delightful. It was as if she was some sort of life-giving nectar that he had to suckle from. He had to taste, lick, bite, kiss.

Inhale her.

He reached the waistline of her jumper and pulled it over her head, then removed the thermal tee shirt she had on underneath that. That was the problem with winter! Too many layers! He couldn't get to her skin quickly enough. He *had* to have her.

All sensible thought had left his head completely. That she was his new colleague. That she was his friend. That maybe there could be a risk in doing this with her and then having to work with her afterwards if it all went wrong.

Who says it's going to go wrong?

None of it mattered any more.

He unclipped her bra as she pulled off his top layers. Their hands were all over each other, and his skin was sizzling at her feathery touch. Cupping her breasts, he lifted her delicate nipples into his mouth and squeezed his eyes shut with ecstasy as she groaned above him, clutching his head, her fingers raking through his hair.

Is there anything sweeter than this?

Pulling Lula to the soft rug in front of the fire, he removed the rest of her clothes. When she'd pulled off his straining trousers she agonisingly kissed his skin, all the way down from his waist, and he thought he would just implode there and then.

When her mouth came back up to his he claimed it once

again with his own, running his hands all over her. Her soft, curvaceous body was lithe and delicate as he pulled himself over her. And he'd been right. There *were* tiny little tattoos all over her. A cute miniature mouse on her hip, a heart in the dimple of her bottom, a trailing sparkle of stars at the top of her thigh…

Condom, Oliver!

'Damn, wait…' He looked for his jacket and saw it over the back of a chair. Leaving her for just a moment, he grabbed his wallet, hoping and praying he had a condom in there.

When had he last needed one?

A while at least…

He couldn't honestly remember if there was one in there!

Oh, thank God!

A small silver packet, tucked behind an old credit card that he never used any more but hadn't bothered to dispose of yet.

Hoping it was in date, he tore at the wrapper with his teeth.

'No. Let me,' she whispered, her breath tickling his chest.

He closed his eyes in agonised lust and tried to gather his control as she slowly and tantalisingly rolled the condom down the length of his penis, almost gasping at the feel of her fingers wrapped tightly around him.

'I want you…' he muttered, but the words didn't mean enough. Not enough to convey just how much he wanted her and needed her right then.

She lay back and smiled at him, reaching out with her hands to pull him down on top of her.

He tortured himself as he deliberately teased her entrance, dying to thrust himself inside her but hesitating, touching briefly, sliding between her folds. Then, unable to hold back any more in case he physically imploded, he entered her. She gasped and grabbed his back, sliding her hands down to his bottom to pull him tighter against her.

Holy mother of...

He didn't want to come straight away. It would have been so easy, but he managed to hold back, enjoying the rise and fall as he moved above her. He crushed her mouth against his as she moaned and groaned. Her fingertips bit into his skin with their nails and all the time his orgasm built up, rising and rising.

Lula writhed beneath him, gasping for air, pulling him towards her, pulling him in deeper, her eyes closed. Her breathing grew faster. Shorter. Then she was crying out, arcing up into his body as he rode her through it.

He moved faster. Harder. He ground himself into her and exploded into a satisfying molten puddle above her as she gasped beneath him. Collapsing, his lips against the skin of her neck, he kissed her one last time, holding on to her, feeling the rise and fall of her chest. Both of them were just breathing, soaking in the moment.

It would have been so easy just to lie there for a while longer. But now that his mind was working clearly again he thought only about getting her to bed. He scooped her up, smiling as she laughed, and made his way up the stairs, kicking open the main bedroom door, shivering slightly at the cold and hurrying them both into bed.

Laughing, they pulled the bedcovers over themselves and snuggled up close, warming each other with their body heat.

Olly held her body against him, kissing her nose, her face, her neck, inhaling her scent once again. It would be so easy for him to take her once again, but he knew there were no more condoms—and he ought to show at least a modicum of self-control.

He felt her remove the condom and groaned at her touch,

knowing he could have no more. Lying in her arms, he fell asleep—only to wake in the early hours feeling guilty.

It was still dark. Olly blinked and turned to see the bedside clock, its digital numerals glowing red in the early hours.

Just gone two o'clock.

His head sank back onto the pillow and he looked at Lula, sleeping peacefully and contentedly beside him.

She was stretched out like a cat, the duvet covering one shoulder, the other bare almost to her breast. He eyed the gentle up-swell of her skin in the dark and remembered how he'd taken her pink nipples in his mouth. Feeling guilty about what he'd done, he pulled the duvet over her shoulder to cover her.

I should never have slept with her. It's Lula, for goodness' sake! My colleague! And she was feeling down. I should never have taken advantage. What does that say about me? What if this changes things between us and makes it awkward?

He'd always thought of himself as an upstanding man. A man who would never take advantage of a woman for his own pleasure. But wasn't that what he'd done with Lula? This whole baby business, the search for her own mother, the Ruby episode—it had all affected her. Made her think about her own situation. It had hit home.

And what did I do?

No clear thinking, that was for sure.

Feeling gutted by his actions, Olly sat up, swinging his legs out of bed. The air was cooler outside of the duvet and all his clothes were still downstairs. Lula hadn't stirred, but he didn't feel he could stay in her bed—not feeling like this—so he got up and padded downstairs, slipping on his clothes as he found them and then building up the fire once again.

He could hear noises, and turned to see Nefertiti and

Cleo looking at him through the bars of their cage, their noses twitching. 'I guess you saw all of that earlier?' he muttered quietly, wondering why on earth he was talking to two rats. 'I admit it—I'm not proud of myself. No matter how lovely your owner is.'

He stood by the cage in two minds. Should he stay? Or go? If he stayed there'd be that awkward morning-after conversation and he didn't think he could bear to go through that. Even if *she* didn't feel awkward, he certainly would. But if he left what would she think of him?

I could leave her a note.

He grabbed some paper and a pen from his grandmother's bureau and scribbled something quickly to imply that he'd got beeped on his pager and would see her later. It seemed the lesser of the two evils, and even though it was a lie he hoped that as it was a white lie it wouldn't hurt her and make her think that he'd abandoned her, too.

There was no way he wanted her to think that. He didn't want to hurt Lula. She was special. She meant something to him. But he thought it was important that they had a proper talk about what happened last night. And the immediate morning after—right before they both had to go to work—wouldn't be the right time.

Pulling on his jacket, he quietly slipped from the cottage, closing the door without making a sound. Standing in the snow outside, he looked up at the bedroom window, imagining himself back beneath the duvet with her.

I wouldn't be able to keep my hands off her!

He wanted her so much! But he also wanted the situation to be right. For her not to be grieving over her mother. For her not to be feeling lost because Ruby had her happy ending and she did not. He didn't want to take advantage of her again.

I hope she doesn't think I used her. I didn't. I wasn't.

Olly sloped away, his feet crunching through the top layer of snow that had begun to freeze overnight.

Lula woke to birdsong. For a long time she just lay there without opening her eyes, feeling content and enjoying the warmth of her bed, remembering the events of the night before. She blinked slowly, thinking she could turn to Olly and hold him before they both had to get up for work.

He wasn't there.

She sat up and looked about the room. No sign of him. But then she remembered they'd stripped each other of their clothes downstairs—perhaps he was down there, making breakfast? She couldn't smell any food. She couldn't hear any sounds.

Was he even there?

He has to be. He wouldn't just disappear in the night, would he?

She got out of her warm bed and slipped on her robe, tying it tightly at the waist before padding downstairs.

'Olly?'

There was no one in the lounge. And no answer to her call.

But there was a note with her name on, propped up on the mantelpiece. Her heart felt heavy as she went over to it, wondering what it might say. Flipping open the paper, she quickly scanned the words and sagged with relief. He'd been paged! Called away in the night to a patient!

She held the note to her chest and beamed. Last night had been amazing! Beautiful and passionate and just what she'd needed. And Olly had been perfect. He'd tasted tantalising. The feel of his strong, broad masculine form encircling her and entering her had made her nerve endings sing like choristers praising God on high with the most beautiful voices.

His very touch had been magical. She'd felt *everything*.

Tingled at every caress, whether with his fingertips or his tongue. She'd almost wanted to consume him. She'd never have guessed it could have been that way with him. Dear Dr Oliver James.

Just thinking about him made her want him again!

But I have to be careful. I'm not meant to be starting something here. I'm here for my mother. That's all. What happened with Olly was fun, but that's all it can be.

She slipped the note into her pocket and went into the kitchen to start breakfast. Anubis sat in his cage, awaiting the sacrifice of some food. She opened the tank's top and dropped in some insects. She kept her hand there, thinking about touching him. Touching that large, plump, hairy body.

Her stomach squirmed, but she knew she had to force herself to try.

She reached down slowly, her breaths long and steady as her nerves shot into overdrive and her flight instinct kicked in. She would have to be gentle. Tarantulas could be damaged by rough handling.

Her fingers were about an inch away and she was just about to touch him…but he moved. Lightning fast she whipped her hand out of the tank, breathing heavily.

Close. So close!

But not yet. Maybe later she'd try again.

The clock in the kitchen told her she had twenty minutes before she needed to be at work. She headed upstairs for a shower.

Lula strode into the surgery, said good morning to the receptionists, and headed off into her room. She switched on the computer system and then went to the staff room to make a cup of coffee.

Whilst she was there Helen, the practice manager, came in, bearing packets of biscuits.

'Oh, they look nice.'

Helen smiled. 'Can't beat a chocolate digestive, I always say.'

'Absolutely. Do you know you can get some with pieces of stem ginger in, too?'

'Ginger's good for you, isn't it?' Helen smirked. 'Might have to get them, then.'

Lula nodded and laughed. 'For medical reasons, yes!' She stirred her tea. 'Do we know what the call-out was last night?'

Helen paused. 'I think it was Mr Levinson. He lives on Old School Road. Chest pains—but it turned out to be indigestion, I think, nothing major.'

She nodded, understanding. 'What time did Olly get called out to him? It must have been in the early hours?'

Helen frowned. 'Olly wasn't on call last night. It was Patrick who went out to the patient.'

'Oh.' Had she misunderstood? Had she read the note wrong? No. Surely not. Olly had been quite clear that he'd been called out to a patient. So why had he written that? Had he *lied*? Had he felt bad about last night and not been able to face her?

Why?

They were both adults. They both knew what they'd done. She knew he was a sensitive soul, but surely he hadn't had second thoughts and run out on her in the middle of the night?

Lula felt as if she'd been kicked in the guts. But not wanting to let her sadness and disappointment show, especially in front of Helen, she forced a smile and went back to her room.

If Olly didn't want to face her then she'd happily give him all the space he needed.

Olly sat in his room, writing up his notes for the last patient he'd seen, but his mind wasn't really on his task. Lula would be here by now. Just down the corridor from him. He could feel her presence, even separated as they were by a few unfeeling walls. She'd not come in to see him—not even to just pop her head round the door and say good morning.

What was going through her mind?

Was she angry with him? No, that couldn't be it. She thought he'd got called out to a patient—there was no reason for her to be angry with him. Perhaps she'd got up late and rushed in, not wanting to be late for work, and just hadn't had the time yet to say hello?

What if she'd not seen his note? That would be awful. She'd think he'd run out on her...

I could go and say hello.

I don't want her to think I'm hiding.

In fact it would be better if I did. Act normal.

He closed the patient's file and headed down the corridor, pausing outside her surgery room. Her name plate practically had an accusing stare and, swallowing down his guilt, he rapped on the door briefly and then opened it.

His beautiful Lula sat behind her desk, her rainbow hair hanging down over her face as she wrote a note, but she looked up at the sound of her door.

'Oh—hi, Olly.'

She didn't seem angry, or mad—or anything, to be honest. He smiled broadly and launched himself further into his lie from last night. 'Sorry I had to leave so quickly last night...'

'Right...that's okay. Sometimes it happens when you're on call.'

Good. She'd got his note. 'I didn't want you to think I'd just left.'

'I didn't.'

'I...er...had a great time last night and...erm...' He stood awkwardly in the doorway, not knowing the best way to finish his sentence. 'I want you to know that it meant a great deal to me, that…erm…that it wasn't just a—' He didn't want to say *one-night stand*. He didn't want to cheapen their experience by saying the words out loud.

'It's fine, Olly. Really. We both wanted it. We're both adults. But it was what it was. Just sex. Nothing more. It doesn't have to affect our work, does it?'

Just sex? *Just?* That hadn't been *just* sex.

'No. Course not. I just wanted to make sure you're okay, that's all. We work together. I don't want it to be awkward, or for there to be an atmosphere.'

Lula beamed him a smile that could have lit a thousand illuminations. 'Of course. Is there anything else?'

How could she be so *normal*? Other women he'd met and had slept with—not that there'd been a lot—had always wanted more commitment from him. Sex had equalled furthering their relationship. Being *in* a relationship, for one thing. Wanting to make sure that he wanted to see them again. That he would be hanging around. That they would continue to go out and be a 'couple'.

But not Lula. She seemed rather blasé about it and he was thrown.

However, he wasn't going to push it. If she wanted that distance between them then he would give it to her. After all, he was the one who had got up in the middle of the early hours of the morning. He was the one who had made up a lie because he'd felt guilty about what he'd done.

I put the surgery and my patients at risk by sleeping with Lula. What if it had caused problems? Where would we have been then? We'd have had to find another locum.

Olly knew he was lying to himself. This wasn't about the surgery. Or the patients. He felt *guilty*. He'd slept with Lula when she'd been feeling vulnerable and now that she was acting as if the sex didn't matter he was protecting himself by telling himself that *she* was the one acting strangely.

It's all my fault.

She was the most beautiful, strange, exotic creature he'd ever met! Last night had been amazing. The caress of her hands on his skin had been mind-blowing. The way her mouth had moved over his body, the way she'd kissed him… It had been like nothing he'd ever experienced before!

I'd love to feel that way again.

But Lula was indicating that it had been nothing more than perfunctory sex. No attachments. Nothing amazing for her. Otherwise she'd want more, wouldn't she?

Like I do?

Nonsense!

Olly slipped from her room and visibly sagged after he'd closed the door behind him. What did he actually want? Lula begging and pleading to see him again? Lula indicating that last night had meant more to her than she was revealing?

That *he* meant something to her?

The idea plagued him. Did he *want* to mean more to Lula?

He ambled back to his own room and sat down in front of the computer. He had patients to see. They were waiting. Sick people—people who needed his help and expertise. Coughing and moaning and staring at the hands on the clock in the waiting room.

That had always mattered to him. He liked to feel needed and valued. He liked the fact that his patients valued his comments and suggestions and came to him for advice.

But not Lula.

The one person I want to want me, doesn't.

He called his next patient through.

Lula sat back in her chair after Olly left and closed her eyes. A headache was beginning to form, tightly furled, like a fist ready to punch her with its might.

She had paracetamol in her handbag and she popped two capsules and swallowed them down with her cold cup of tea from earlier.

Why did I pretend everything was all right?

She didn't want Olly to think of her as a woman who just slept with a man casually, as if it meant nothing. Because she wasn't like that. Lula Chance did *not* just sleep with men for fun. The last time she'd slept with a man had been years ago. And that had been in a relationship—nothing casual about it at all.

Being with Olly last night *had* meant something. She'd welcomed his arms around her, his lips on hers, the feel of his broad, masculine body above hers, moving within her, bringing her to the release that she'd needed. There'd been a connection. It had meant something.

The last two days with Ruby and the baby had hit her hard. It had brought forward a lot of emotions she'd thought she'd stamped down. For some reason all those feelings she'd fought for so long had become powerful and raw. Maybe it was because she felt so close to finding her own mother. Or perhaps it was just being here in Atlee Wold with Olly and his wonderful father, seeing how close they were as a family. Her emotions were exposed to the elements and the winter freeze had crystallised them and made them difficult to deal with.

And Olly...lovely, lovely Olly. His twinkling eyes and warm smile and the way he cared had somehow broken through her defences, making her crave things she'd always denied herself.

She'd never meant to get involved with anyone. Why *do* that? Get involved romantically when it could only end badly? Infertility was a big enough burden for her—why force it on to someone else? Why go through all that? Tests and hormones and needles—God, the needles! She'd seen enough of those in her life. Felt the stress, the humiliation of feeling *less* than other women.

Women had babies. It was their primary function, wasn't it? They were the only people who could carry a baby, so that was what they were meant to do.

What did you do with your life if you couldn't even do that?

Her life had already been blighted with cancer, and chemotherapy had made her infertile. She'd decided long ago that she wouldn't burden anyone else with those concerns. What kind of life would that give them? No, Lula did enough worrying for two as it was.

Her life was about adventure and travel and meeting new people—experiencing everything the world had to offer until the day came when she couldn't do it any more.

It was *not* about moving to a small, quaint English village and falling for the local GP!

Have I fallen for Olly?

No. Of course not. That was ridiculous! She hadn't known him very long, and one night of sex didn't create serious feelings.

So why do I feel so upset that he lied about last night?

Lula sat there, feeling the edges of the headache prowling around her. She couldn't even see the pen she was twiddling in her fingers—she was thinking too hard about Olly and how he made her feel.

I can't get attached. I have to keep my distance, I'm not staying here.

Perhaps she needed to plan her next step? Forget Olly, forget how he'd made her feel last night, and especially forget how she'd felt waking up this morning to find him gone. There was no point in dwelling on that. No point in thinking about how much she'd looked forward to coming downstairs and finding him sitting in her kitchen, waiting to kiss her good morning.

I've never had that anyway, so I won't miss it.

Sleeping with Olly had been a mistake, no matter how much she'd enjoyed it or how much she craved more of the same. Not just the sex, but the feeling of closeness. The bonding they'd shared just for a few hours…

Stop it!

She had to think of it as a mistake. If she didn't she'd go insane. She couldn't have Olly. He wanted a different future from the one she could provide.

I am not here for anything else but finding my mother.

That was what her coming to Atlee Wold was all about. Finding her mother at last. Learning the truth about her past and then moving on to experience the next thing. Maybe keeping in contact with her mother if she wished it.

Lula looked at the names on the piece of paper in front of her.

Eleanor Lomax.

Elizabeth Love.

Edward Loutham.

The Louthams had to be ruled out, didn't they? Bonnie had said that there was only Edward Loutham with an 'E' name in that family, as far as she knew. And even she didn't think that her mother had changed sex and fathered some children!

So he's ruled out.

That left two names. Two women. One of whom she'd met in Olly's surgery.

Eleanor Lomax.

The woman who'd survived breast cancer. The woman with a sister called Brenda in the next village over.

Lula thought back to their meeting. Eleanor had been very elegant. Silver-haired already, so Lula had no idea if her original hair colour had been dark like her own. But their eyes were the same colour. Was that enough to go on? She'd said she took care of herself. Didn't like to lean on anyone else for help. Much like Lula. Was that enough?

Then there was the enigmatic Elizabeth Love. A woman Olly didn't know much about. A woman who apparently ran an animal sanctuary and kept herself to herself.

I know nothing else about her. I don't even know what she looks like. I'm really chasing my own tail here.

It was frustrating. To be so close and yet so far. And the other thing Lula had to consider was that *neither* of those women had anything to do with her! They might just be complete strangers. Random women with the same initials as a woman who'd once written something in a letter. Even those initials could have been fake. Something to throw people off the trail.

What if I'm chasing smoke? What if my mother never even came from here and in reality I'm miles away from finding out the truth?

Lula groaned and put the paper back in her pocket. Then she took it back out again. There really was nothing else for her to go on. If she didn't check out these two leads then she'd never forgive herself.

Lula found the women's addresses on the surgery's system and went online to look at a street map of Atlee Wold. Eleanor Lomax lived just down the road from the surgery on Church Drive. Elizabeth Love lived out on Burner's Road, just down from the farm. She'd need to drive to that one.

Eleanor first, then.

She picked up her phone, pressing nine for an outside line, and dialled Eleanor's number. It was answered quickly.

'Hello?'

'Miss Lomax?'

'Yes?'

'Hello, there. My name's Dr Chance. I'm calling from

the local surgery. I sat in with you and Dr James during your consultation the other day.'

'Oh…yes…is something wrong?'

'No—no! I just…erm…well, I wondered whether I might pop round after lunch and see you?'

There was a pause. 'What about?'

Lula felt awkward. 'It's a private matter. I'd prefer to discuss it in person, if that's okay?'

There was a sound of irritation, and then, 'I suppose so. But I'm going out at two o'clock—you'll have to be quick.'

Lula had seen all her morning patients. 'Could I come round now?'

Eleanor agreed and Lula said goodbye and grabbed her coat. Church Drive wasn't far—she'd walk.

She let the practice manager know she was popping out briefly. 'But I'll be back in about an hour if you want to prepare the home visit list.' It was Lula's turn to do the home visits on her own.

She was just about to escape the surgery when Olly's door opened and he instantly spotted her, dressed in her coat, hat and boots.

'Going somewhere?'

Lula didn't want to discuss the matter in front of the others, so she went over to him and whispered, 'I'm going to see Eleanor Lomax.'

He stared deep into her eyes and she felt guilty for trying to sneak away.

'I'll come with you.'

'You've got patients.'

'I've just finished. Let me grab my coat.'

She waited, feeling awkward and unsure. She'd wanted to do this alone, but he seemed determined to tag along. She couldn't fault him for trying to help her, but she'd really wanted to sneak away. Get some distance between her and Olly so she could make plans to finalise her departure from Atlee Wold.

Out in the snow, she buttoned up her coat, enjoying the bright morning sunshine on her face. As they walked past gardens she could actually see evidence of melting. Icicles dripped and more bushes and greenery could be seen than a few days ago.

'Spring's coming, don't you think?' Olly asked.

'There's definitely a thaw.'

Lula loved the snow, but hated slush, and she hoped that if it were all about to melt it would do so quickly. No point in making everywhere a mess.

They passed a red-breasted robin, perched on a stone wall, and then the church and graveyard, with the old stones sticking up from the ground like teeth.

Soon they were standing outside Eleanor's door, ringing the bell, their noses red from the cold.

Eleanor answered, looking cosy in a mohair jumper, skirt and thick tights, a string of pearls about her neck.

'Oh, I wasn't expecting both of you. Come in.'

She walked them through to her lounge and Lula looked about for clues. Pictures—anything that might indicate that this woman's past was connected to hers. But there was nothing. Eleanor's furniture was expensive, and beautifully chosen, but the only pictures about the place were works by artists: hunting scenes, a landscape, a kingfisher perched above a river.

'So—I'm intrigued. What's this all about? Is it my cancer?'

Lula shook her head. 'Nothing to do with your health. Not now. This is awkward, but I'd like you to bear with me.'

'Go on.' Eleanor sat opposite, her hands clasped neatly on her lap, her back as erect as it had been in the surgery.

'This is about *me*, really, Miss Lomax.'

'Call me Eleanor, dear.'

'Eleanor. I'm just a locum here, as you know, but I'm not only here in Atlee Wold to work. I'm here to…to search for my mother.'

Eleanor was listening, but her face showed nothing. No surprise, no awkwardness, no indication that long ago she'd had a secret child and abandoned her on a beach.

'I believe my mother is in this village. She left a letter, signing it with the initials EL, and I think she was from Atlee Wold. I'm trying to track her down.'

The older woman frowned for a moment, then her eyebrows were raised. 'You think…? EL…? You think it might be me? Oh, dear! I can assure you it's not.'

Lula felt Olly look at her and could almost physically feel his sympathy radiating from across the room.

She must have visibly sagged in her seat, for Eleanor continued, 'I'm so sorry to disappoint you, Dr Chance, but I'm not the lady you're looking for.'

Lula bit her lip and cast her gaze down to the floor. 'Have you always lived here, Eleanor?'

'I was born in the back room—so, yes, I have.'

'Do you recall anyone getting pregnant and going away? Coming back without a baby?'

Eleanor shook her head and was silent for a moment. 'Many things have happened here in Atlee Wold in my lifetime. I can't be expected to remember everything. Maybe… I don't know…'

'If I asked you about…someone else…would you tell me what you know?'

'It depends on who it is, my dear. I might know nothing, and even if I did would it be my secret to tell? I'm not sure that would be right of me.'

Lula nodded. 'I appreciate that.'

'Who do you want to know about?'

'You might not know her. Apparently she keeps herself

to herself. Even Dr James knows nothing about her. Elizabeth Love? On Burner's Road?'

Eleanor took in a deep breath. 'I know Lizzy. We used to go to school together.'

Lula sat up again on the edge of her seat. 'You did?'

'I haven't seen her for years, though. You're right about her hiding away. She prefers to talk to her animals and most people round here call her Dr Dolittle. I've seen her once or twice, picking up groceries in the village shop, but it's just an acknowledgement. We don't stand and talk.'

'Why not?'

Eleanor shrugged. 'I'm not sure. I left the village school aged fourteen to go to secretarial college and she dropped off my radar, to be honest. She was a good friend. A nice girl. Bit too trusting, but she was nice. You think she might be your mother?'

'I don't know. She's the only other EL in the village that I could find on the electoral roll. Unless you know of any others?'

Eleanor glanced at her watch. 'I don't. And I'm afraid I'm going to have to rush you away. I have an appointment.'

Lula nodded and stood up. So now Eleanor Lomax was crossed off the list. All she had left was Elizabeth Love as a possibility, and if that was wrong, too…

Where would she go from there? There was nowhere else *to* go. She could contact the Salvation Army, maybe, or see if Social Services had any records on her, but the chances of finding her mother would be slim.

Outside, Olly laid his hand on hers. 'I'm so sorry.'

She shrugged. 'It's not your fault, is it?'

'No. But I still wish I could make you feel better.'

Oh, he could. By taking her in his arms and kissing her, smothering her with his mouth and his body, pulling at her clothes and taking her madly, as he'd never taken anyone before… But that wasn't going to happen.

Lula looked up at his bright blue eyes. 'I need to find her, Olly.'

A gloved finger stroked her cheek. 'I know.'

She wanted to kiss him then. Wanted it more than she'd ever wanted to do anything in the whole wide world. But she couldn't. She needed to separate from him. Stop relying on him to make her feel better.

I'm a lone spirit. I take care of myself.

Back at the surgery, Lula made herself a fresh cup of tea and sat in the staffroom, mulling over the events of the last few days. She couldn't call Elizabeth. She didn't have a number listed in the surgery records. All she could do was turn up unannounced and hope for the best.

But I've had enough disappointment for today. Maybe I'll do it tomorrow. It might have thawed some more and it'll be easier to park Betsy.

Do I want to go alone?

For some reason Lula felt as if this was her last-ditch attempt at trying to track down her mother, and that she'd like some moral support. That would be okay, wouldn't it? Would Olly go with her? Or maybe his father? All she needed was a friend.

No. She wanted Olly with her. It felt right—especially after the closeness they'd shared.

She took her tea to his room to ask him, but he'd gone. Disappointed, needing to see his smiling face, she decided to pop round to his house and ask him personally if he'd go with her tomorrow. There was no harm in that, was there? It was the sort of favour you'd ask of a friend, and if Olly was anything to her he was most definitely a friend.

Because I can't have him any other way.

CHAPTER SEVEN

IT WAS THE first time she'd been to Olly's home. He lived in a quaint house made of grey stone that sat on the end of a long terrace.

She rang the doorbell and waited, ignoring the cold that was seeping through her boots and into her toes. It wasn't as bad as the other day, when she'd slipped into the icy water, but it was getting there.

The door opened and Olly stood there, a smile on his face. 'Lula! I wasn't expecting you. Something wrong with the home visit rota?'

'No, no…I just wondered if I might ask you a favour?'

He nodded, then stepped back, welcoming her in, and she entered the house, enjoying the rich warmth inside. As she passed the living room she saw a large open fire, already lit, crackling and spitting its way through the logs. Then she followed him into the kitchen.

It was in an old style, full of faded beech, and the walls were painted a soft green. Copper-bottomed pans hung from the ceiling above a central breakfast bar, where he appeared to have been chopping some vegetables.

'I'm sorry if I've interrupted your lunch.'

'These are for this evening's casserole. Would you like to join us?'

It was a nice offer, but she didn't want to intrude on him any more than she already had done. He'd made it clear by leaving her after their passionate encounter, and then lying about his reasons for doing so, that he didn't want to get too involved with her.

'No, no, I wouldn't dream of—'

'It's not a problem. There's plenty, and Dad would love to catch up with you.'

Patrick would like to catch up with her? Not Olly? Another sign…

'Well, thank you.'

'You're happy with lamb?'

She nodded. It was her favourite.

'Drink? Tea? Coffee?'

'No, thanks. I just popped round to ask you a quick question.'

He stopped his chopping to focus on her and she found herself feeling awkward beneath his soft blue gaze. 'You know I'm still looking for my mother?'

Olly nodded.

'I want to speak to Elizabeth Love. She's my only lead left and I'm kind of nervous about that.'

He nodded his head slowly. 'When are you going to speak to her?'

'Tomorrow. And that's what I'm here for. I'd really feel better about going if you were with me. For moral support. But if you don't want to I don't want you to feel forced to do it.'

'Why wouldn't I want to support you?' He sounded genuinely perplexed by her explanation.

She looked away from his steely gaze, shrugging. 'Just… you know…last night… And now I'm asking you to maybe come and find my mother with me… I wouldn't want you to think I was pushing you into getting more involved with my circumstances than you need to be.'

'Lula, I'd *love* to help you. This is a big thing. Last

night was…' he looked uncomfortable '…was something we should never have done.'

Lula stood looking at him across the breakfast bar, shocked to hear him actually say it to her. She'd assumed he'd try to skirt the issue. 'Right…no…that's fine. I understand. I mean, me, too… I don't want to get romantically involved with anyone, you know…' Her sentence drifted off into nothing.

He stepped around the bar towards her. 'In fact I'd like to apologise. I should never have slept with you. Not that I didn't want to! I did, and you were amazing. But…you were vulnerable and upset. I should never have taken advantage.'

He was standing very close to her now and she could smell his scent. A masculine scent of musk and something like sandalwood. It was delicious.

'Advantage? No, Olly, you didn't. I wanted it just as much as you did.' She frowned. 'Is that why you pretended you got a call-out?'

His cheeks flushed and he took a step back. 'You know?'

Lula smiled and nodded. 'I found out this morning. I thought you'd had second thoughts, but I wasn't sure why. Not that it matters anyway. We're both consenting adults. We both enjoyed it.'

Just talking about it brought memories of their night rushing back into her head. The heat. The way he'd moved above her. The way he'd touched her, kissed her, his mouth nibbling and licking in all the right places…

Lula flushed with need but, unable to pursue it, looked down at the floor to try and gain some control over her feelings and thoughts. She would have given anything to enjoy those sensations again, but she wouldn't allow herself.

Olly looked as if he was struggling to speak. His mouth opened as if he was about to say something, then closed as his gaze roamed over her, his blue eyes sparkling with hunger for her.

'So…you'll come with me? Tomorrow?' She looked back at him, in control once more.

'Sure.'

'And I'll come for dinner tonight?'

He nodded. 'About seven?'

Lula smiled. Yes. That was fine.

'Dad goes out after dinner on a Thursday night.'

Of course—it was Thursday! She had another belly-dancing class at six! 'I might be a little late. My class runs till seven o'clock, and then I'll have to lock up.'

'It'll keep for when you get here.'

Their gazes locked and they stood there for some time. Neither of them moving forward. Neither of them moving away. Just looking at each other, lost in their own emotions and needs.

Eventually the sound of the kitchen clock ticking away made her return to the here and now. 'I'll get going, then.'

Olly followed her to the front door.

She wasn't sure whether to kiss him goodbye or not, but she couldn't resist. What harm could one goodbye kiss do? She stood on tiptoe, closing her eyes as she planted her lips on his cheek. For a moment she hovered there, her eyes still closed, inhaling the scent of him, debating whether she should kiss him properly—especially when she felt him brush his lips over the side of her mouth.

How easy it would be to turn her head…so tempting!

Instead, she lowered herself off her tiptoes and stepped back, smiling. 'Well, I'll see you.'

'Right.' He looked disappointed. 'Have you got many house calls to make?'

'Three. I'm on my way now.'

'Want company?'

Yes, she did. Olly's company would be nice right now. But was it fair to ask him to go with her? It was only three house calls, and he'd done his fair share of them for some time whilst the practice had searched for a locum. She wanted to pull her own weight properly, but she didn't want to offend him by saying no.

'That's up to you. I don't mind. I'm happy to do them on my own.'

'I'll grab my coat.' He reached for his jacket and shrugged it over his shoulders, then stuck his feet into some tough-looking hiking boots and tied the laces. 'Ready when you are.'

She went outside to her car and heard his steps falter as they neared the spotted Betsy.

'Ah, I forgot about her.' He grinned ruefully.

Lula smiled at his amusement. 'How could you ever forget Betsy? There aren't that many cars painted like a lady-bird, you know.' She slid in the driver's side and leant over to pop his door open. When he got in she had to fight the urge to lean over and kiss him. It was what she wanted to do. Wanted very much indeed. But she knew it wouldn't be right and she started the engine, determined not to think about the way he kissed. Or touched. Or made her feel.

How could he have disrupted her state of mind so much? He was just an ordinary man, like any other. Wasn't he? And though it might be fun and sexy and irresistible with him right now, as time went by the situation most certainly would change. There would have to be commitment and, Olly being Olly, he would undoubtedly start to want children. He was traditional that way. And she couldn't give him that. Nor did she want to go through the pain of splitting up with him. She'd been there, done that, and it had been hard and disruptive.

Best to keep things light and fun. They could have fun, right? Without it becoming too serious?

'So, who's first?'

She passed him the list. 'Karen Harper. What do you know about her?'

'Karen? She's a lovely old lady. She was at your dance class the other week.'

'Which one was she?'

'A few rows back from the front? Black leotard with pink leggings?' He smiled at the memory.

Lula nodded. She remembered her. She'd been the only lady there in a leotard—all the others had turned up in tee shirts or tracksuits. And the bright pink leggings had revealed a very good pair of shapely legs for an elderly lady. Lula had liked her. She'd really embraced the class and laughed and had fun.

'Apparently she's taken a fall in the snow and thinks she's sprained her ankle. She doesn't want to go to hospital to have it checked and couldn't make it in to the surgery for us to check it. Shame. Probably means she won't be at my class tonight.'

'You know she once made a play for my father?'

Lula glanced at him as she drove through the slush. 'Really?'

'He let her down very gently. There's never been anyone else for him apart from my mother.'

'He loved your mum very much?'

'She was an amazing woman.'

'I thought you didn't remember her?'

'I don't, but my father has told me so much about her I feel as if I do.'

Lula nodded in understanding. 'No wonder you have a list of attributes for your ideal woman. You're looking for what your father had.'

She felt him looking at her and burned beneath his gaze. 'That's deep. I didn't know you had psychology training as well as training in general practice.'

Lula laughed gently. 'I took a side class.'

He was quiet for a moment, then spoke again, his voice low. 'Perhaps you're right. When my dad speaks of her he gets this faraway look in his eyes and he goes all wistful. And he talks of her so…lovingly. Like she was perfect, you know? I'm sure they must have had their moments when they couldn't even look at each other, but the way he tells it…she was everything.'

Lula said nothing. Neither of them had had a mother. It was something they shared in common, even if for different reasons. She knew how much it had hurt *her* not to have a mother. Or a father, for that matter. She'd felt lost and rootless and unwanted as a little girl—had often felt that she had no value whatsoever. And at senior school she'd been picked on because of it. Kids had called her 'Annie' after the most famous orphan of Broadway. Lula had hated it and had been angry at a mother she didn't have for putting her through it.

How had it been for Olly? He had a mother he couldn't remember. One who had died unexpectedly in a tragic accident before her time. He couldn't get his mother back, but she might find hers. There was still an opportunity for her to build bridges. Or at least she hoped so. What would it be like to lose her forever?

As she pulled up in front of Karen's house she got out of the car and looked at him across the roof of Betsy. 'There's someone out there. For you. Someone who's perfect.'

He frowned. 'So it's not you, then?'

Lula stopped in her tracks.

No! I can't let it be me!

'I'm not the marrying kind, and you're after someone who wants to take a short walk down a church aisle and into a maternity unit.'

She turned away before he could answer her. But he caught up with her before she was halfway up the pathway.

'Who's to say that's what I want?'

She looked at his hand gripping her arm. 'Of *course* it's what you want. You've been telling yourself that for years.'

He let go. 'It's different now.'

'Why?'

'Because I met you.'

The intensity in his eyes frightened her. She pushed past him and rang the doorbell, her heart thundering away in her chest and her stomach rolling and dipping like a ship on a stormy sea.

They headed into Karen's house. She was surprised to see two doctors turn up for her sprained ankle. They strapped her ankle and advised her to rest, then spent their next two visits keeping their conversation light and non-committal.

It was getting awkward. Already.

Lula grimaced her way through the afternoon, determined more than ever that she was right to keep her distance from Olly.

The casserole was simmering nicely, and rich, meaty smells filled the James household. Patrick had opened a bottle of red and prepared a selection of soft drinks for Lula, who was on call that evening.

She arrived about fifteen minutes late and drifted into Olly's kitchen wearing her belly-dancing paraphernalia. Once again he was treated to the sight of her trim waist, with her belly button jewel twinkling in the firelight. Her bangles clinked and jingled, giving off a musical noise every time she moved, and she wore the most amazing skirt, that appeared to be made of some sort of wafting fabric that floated about her body as she walked.

He tried not to stare, but it was difficult.

'You're going to be on call wearing *that*?'

He could just imagine the reactions of some of the elderly male patients when she turned up wearing a skirt with a huge split up the side. He remembered what it had felt like to slide his fingers up the length of her legs and had to swallow hard and pretend he was checking the roast potatoes in the oven.

Since last night he'd not been able to think straight. She was in his head no matter which way he turned. She was at work, she was in his home, but always just out of reach. And he was sensing she really wanted to keep him there. Out of reach. And here she was again, looking all petite and beautiful and alluring, and all he could think of was sweeping her up into his arms and whisking her away up the stairs. Leaving his dad to eat the casserole alone whilst he and Lula enjoyed each other once more.

And it wasn't just the sex, he kept telling himself. It was Lula herself. She had no idea how amazing she was—the type of person she was. Her quirky traits, her unique look. They were all things he would never have normally been attracted to, but with Lula it was different. He *was* attracted to her—there was no denying that. There were strong feelings—he couldn't help those, either—but she was keeping him at a distance and he wasn't sure why.

There were the obvious reasons, of course. They were work colleagues. They were in a small village where gossip ran rife, and neither of them needed to be the main topic on the Atlee Wold grapevine.

But he sensed there was something more and he couldn't quite grasp it.

Was she being the sensible one? Last night had been amazing, and even though he felt guilty about taking advantage it hadn't stopped him craving her touch once again. They'd shared a lingering kiss, but she'd been quick to say they were both adults, that she wasn't his type, that she would never marry, and that he was after some sort of traditional wife.

Why did she always bring it back to that? As if a woman being a wife and mother were the only things that mattered to him?

Because it wasn't just that. Maybe he'd once thought so, but Rachel had changed all that. Having an abortion without telling him she'd even been pregnant, and then walking out on him without giving him a chance to say goodbye or even discuss why they were breaking up.

It had caused him to rethink life. And, yes, he'd been playing it safe—because by doing that he'd thought he could control the outcome. If he went out with someone who was a safe option then he wouldn't get hurt.

That was the basics of it.

He didn't want the pain he'd experienced before. He didn't want the agony of that.

And Lula wasn't a safe option. She was her own person—bright, funny, a risk-taker, a challenger of the norms, someone who'd made no promises to stay.

But Lula also had a way of changing the world. Even his dad had said so.

She looked down at herself, removing the coin-edged skirt that had been moulding the soft curve of her bottom, letting loose the floaty fabric that caressed the length of her legs.

'No—sorry. Can I pop upstairs to get changed? I didn't get time at the hall.'

'Of course.'

Patrick led her upstairs to show her where to get changed and Olly watched them go, jealous of how his dad's hand rested so easily—unthinkingly—in the small of Lula's back.

Jealous? He blinked the feeling away and concentrated on preparing the gravy for the meal. Why was he jealous? That was his *father*, for crying out loud! Lula hadn't committed to Olly, had she? It was her quintessential spirit of being free and life-affirming that intrigued him. She had no roots. Well, not yet. She might find some tomorrow, if Elizabeth Love was the woman she was looking for.

And what then? Surely if Elizabeth *was* Lula's mother then Lula would stay in Atlee Wold? And if she stayed there'd be a chance for him to be with her?

But what if Elizabeth *wasn't* her mother? Would Lula stay?

He endeavoured to ask her at some point. Maybe when his father left later and they were alone together.

Lula came downstairs wearing gorgeous tight black jeans and an off-the-shoulder red top. He tried not to look at the delicate dip where her neck met her chest, or at the long, slow curve of her collarbone. She'd enjoyed him kissing her there…

He blinked and offered her a drink. She took an orange juice and sat at the table as he served up.

'So, were there many at your class this evening?' he asked.

She nodded. 'Yes, I'm pleased to say. Three more people than last time.'

'That's good,' Patrick interjected. 'You've really aroused the spirit of the older generation in this village, Lula. You're just what *some* people needed.' He glanced at his son across the table. 'A breath of fresh air.'

She smiled and thanked him for his compliment.

'It's true, my dear! Even my Oliver has perked up since your arrival. For a long time I thought the poor lad was going to end up just like me.'

Olly looked at his father. 'What's wrong with being like you?'

'Nothing—if having a limited world is what you want. If Atlee Wold is to be the centre of your universe. There's such a big world out there, son, and I've always wanted you to experience it.'

It was the first time he'd heard his father speak like this.

'I know you felt a great sense of pressure about coming into the practice. Because of me and your grandad before you. If you wanted to do that, that's fine. But I'd really like to think there's more out there for you.'

'Dad, I—'

'It's okay, son. You'll never disappoint me.'

Olly looked stuck for something to say. His father's comments had come out of the blue.

Patrick smiled, a twinkle in his eyes. 'Can't a father look out for his son? Well, *I* can. Especially when I can see what's good for you.' He turned to Lula. 'Although I, for one, hope that *you* consider staying on in Atlee Wold, Lula.'

Lula didn't appear to be blushing, but she did seem pleased at his father's words.

'I haven't made any definite plans yet, Patrick.'

Olly pulled the casserole pot from the oven and set it in the centre of the table, removing the lid, allowing a plume of steam to swirl up to the ceiling and mouth-watering aromas to set them all salivating.

They set to the meal readily, all of them hungry, and pretty soon there were three empty plates and three full bellies. Patrick went into the living room whilst Olly and Lula cleared away the dishes. She scraped and rinsed the plates, and he set them in the dishwasher.

'Thanks, but you're meant to be my guest—not helping me do domestic duties.'

'Oh, I'm not afraid to get my hands dirty.'

He agreed. She'd certainly not shirked any work since she'd been here. 'How are you feeling about tomorrow? Nervous?'

Lula nodded. 'A bit. Everything could change, couldn't it?'

'And if she *is* your mother? What then?'

Lula stood still, her hands dripping water, before drying them on a towel. 'I don't allow myself to think that far ahead.'

'But you must have imagined it? Finding her?'

'Yes, but I find if I try and imagine a conversation it never goes the way I heard it in my mind and I don't want to be disappointed.'

No. He hated to think of her being upset. Devastated and crying. Just the idea of it set his stomach churning and had him fighting the urge to hold her. He wanted to wrap his arms around her and hold her close. Protect her from anything that could do her harm—emotionally or physically.

'What time shall we go over there?'

'Well, your dad has the morning surgery, so I thought about ten? We should be back for the afternoon surgery, then, with plenty of time.'

'I hope you get what you want, Lula. I hope you find her.'

Lula looked at him steadily. He could see that her eyes were glazed, almost as if she might be about to cry. How easy it would be to take a step past the open dishwasher and hold her!

'Thank you, Olly.'

They finished off in the kitchen and went into the living room to have coffee with Patrick. Then Patrick said goodnight to them both and went off to meet up with his friends down at the local pub.

When he was gone Lula sat next to Olly on the couch, staring into the open fire. There was something hypnotic about the flames. Something soothing. And somehow, without realising how it came to happen, he realised that he had his arm about her shoulders and she was leaning into his chest.

She was a comforting weight against him and he looked down at her, staring at her amazing hair and at how all the colours blended so beautifully into one another, and how the firelight flickered and played off them. He could inhale the scent of her shampoo...

I could take her face in my hand and turn her to kiss me...

She turned and looked at him, startling him with the

intensity in her eyes. It was almost magical, as if she'd heard his thoughts and granted his wishes. They said no words. They didn't have to. He could read everything he needed to in her beautiful large brown eyes. Pools of molten chocolate he would happily swim in...

He couldn't help himself... His gaze dropped to her lips. Her beautiful lips. Full and sensuously curved. Bubblegum pink and innately kissable...

He lowered his face to hers and saw her eyes close as she welcomed his mouth on hers. Their kiss was of exquisite beauty. Her lips melted against his and he felt her fingers in his hair. He heard her soft sigh as she turned to press herself against him.

Heat fired instantly in his groin and he fought its desire for instant gratification. He told himself that this time he would take it slowly and enjoy each delicious moment they were together. He'd sensed her trying to put distance between them. Sensed her stepping away. Well, if this was the last time he'd get to be with her then he was going to treasure every moment...

His arms held her tightly against him and her breathing became heavy. Their kisses deepened and he found himself stroking her skin, allowing his hands to roam her body. Their clothes were in the way. He wanted to touch her skin.

He wanted *her*. Not just in a physical sense. It was more than just sex. It was almost about consuming her. Touching, tasting, feeling everything that she was. Absorbing her into his very being.

Lula leaned back and pulled off her top, then began to tackle his shirt buttons. His mouth dropped to the gentle swell of her breasts, to the pert, taut nipples peaking beneath the lace of her bra.

How easy it would be just to rip it away...

Olly restrained himself, however. His fingers found the clip at the back and released it. The bra hit the floor and his hands cupped her, brought her to his mouth. His tongue teased and licked and his teeth nibbled gently, causing pain and pleasure at the same time, and her groans were like music to his ears. He filled his mouth with her.

She pulled off his shirt and began tackling his trousers. He tried to undo her jeans, but they were so tight they both stopped to laugh as she helped him undo them, and then they, too, were off and discarded upon the floor.

Olly gazed at the beautiful length of her. At her sex obscured by a small piece of flimsy red lace. She was amazing. Gorgeous. If he had an artistic bone in his body he would want to draw her, paint her as she lay in repose. Each brushstroke an imagined caress. That way he could look at her like that for as long as he wanted.

But she held out her arms, drawing him to her, and he fell upon her like a rabid wolf, his mouth consuming her, ravishing her, tasting her flesh and her scent as he peeled away the wisp of lacy underwear.

And there she lay. His beautiful Lula. Naked in his living room before the open fire. His mouth met hers once again. Her groaning almost sent him over the edge. He wanted her so badly.

He felt her flesh slip and slide beneath his touch, her nipples hardening as she ground herself against him, and then she gasped, arching her back, clutching herself against him, and he just knew in his heart that he wanted to experience that with her again and again and again.

She'd got beneath his skin…there was no denying it.

She was his beautiful, amazing Lula Chance, and if he got to be with her every day and know that she was his every night then he would be a very happy man.

Was it love? He didn't know. Maybe. It had happened quickly, if it was. He'd only ever committed himself like that to someone once before, and that had been a long time ago. So he wasn't sure, but he thought that maybe it did feel that way.

The last time he'd fallen in love it had been a disaster. He'd convinced himself that Rachel was the woman for him—perfect in every way, the perfect partner for a country village GP—but she hadn't been. He'd imposed his own expectations on to her and thought she would be what he wanted her to be. But she'd had other ideas. She'd been a free spirit, very much a city girl who didn't want to be tied down, the way he'd expected.

And wasn't Lula the same? A free spirit who might leave him?

Dismissing the doubt, he slid into her all the way, feeling her heat along the length of him, the taste of her still on his tongue, her soft skin beneath his fingers. He moved gently. Slowly at first, then quicker and harder, until the breath was escaping from him in bursts. He came in a shattering gasp, collapsing on top of her, his breath at her neck—her delicious neck, with that gentle dip and the collarbone that had intrigued him so much earlier.

It had been every bit as amazing as before. If not better.

I can't let her go.

But he still wasn't sure if she was his to keep.

They lay in each other's arms, content. Neither saying what they truly needed to say. Both knowing that this might be the last time they were together.

Elizabeth Love's house sat centrally in a square plot, surrounded by sheds and aviaries and outdoor hutches, all filled with animals of various kinds. Loose chickens and ducks roamed the gardens.

The gate to the garden path hung limply and rusting, off to one side. As the snow had now melted somewhat the ground beneath was starting to be seen—thick mud, almost black, but by the front door a cornucopia of clay pots held flowering snowdrops and crocus.

Lula smiled at Olly nervously and then took a step forward and rapped on the door. Some old flaking paint fell off at her touch, revealing the ancient, grey wood beneath, whilst the free-ranging chickens scratched at her feet.

The sun was shining and there was warmth in its gaze. Finally, it seemed, the snow would soon be gone.

Lula waited, Olly standing a little behind her. There'd been no awkwardness since last night. After she and Olly had made love they'd cuddled before the fire for a while, until she'd realised she needed to go home before Patrick came back and found them naked in his lounge! She'd dressed quickly and kissed him goodbye.

It had been fun to share that time with him, but that was all it could be. At least that was what she kept telling herself. It had been hard to leave his warm, strong arms. Difficult to walk away from him. They'd grown so close over the last few days together.

But that was all it was. Two adults who were good friends and occasionally had sex. That was all. No strings, no demands from either side. Friends with benefits. If it ended tomorrow and they just stayed as friends after that there'd be no recriminations from either side. She hoped he felt the same way. She'd indicated nothing else, even if she hadn't said it out loud. And he knew she never stayed anywhere for longer than a few months. That she always moved on. That she always sought something new. He had to know that was how it was going to end.

She was pulled from her thoughts when the door was opened by a small woman. She had dark hair, slightly tinted with grey at the front, and large brown eyes. She wore a comfortable, hard-wearing flannel shirt with jeans, boots and no make-up.

Lula smiled a greeting, then faltered as the sunlight

caught on the silver necklace that hung at the woman's throat. It was the same as the necklace that Lula wore. The one she'd been left with by her mother.

The woman blinked at the bright sun, looking at them both enquiringly. 'Yes?'

Lula's voice caught in her throat. 'Miss Love?'

'Yes?'

'I'm Dr Chance, and this is Dr James from the local surgery. May we come in for a moment and talk to you?'

'What about? I'm busy.' Elizabeth's harsh response was clipped and fast.

Lula looked at the hard lines on this woman's face and saw a lifetime of heartache. 'It's a private matter.'

'I'm sure I have nothing worth discussing…'

The woman went to shut the door and Lula just stood there, but Olly stepped forward, jutting his boot into the doorway, his broad, square hand pressed against the door.

'It's about your daughter, Miss Love.'

The woman flinched visibly, staring at them both, then her eyes flicked to Lula, assessing her. Her gaze softened.

Lula stood there, letting her look, wondering what she was thinking. Wondering whether she'd guessed yet who she was. Whether she saw the similarities. Elizabeth Love had the same eyes as her.

'You'd better come in.' She stepped away and disappeared down a dark hall that was overflowing with piles of stuff.

Lula had seen television programmes about hoarders before, and though this house wasn't as bad as some of them she could tell that this woman didn't like to let things go. It was cluttered, and it wasn't very clean, but there was organisation here—and a love for animals that was clear for anyone to see.

Elizabeth indicated for them to sit down on the cat-

covered sofa opposite, then sat herself, fidgeting and twist-
ing the tails of her shirt in her fingertips. 'Well?'

Lula swallowed hard. She'd found her. This *had* to be
her mother! 'We're here to talk about a baby girl who was
left abandoned on a beach many years ago.'

'I see.' She didn't meet their eyes, but kept her gaze cast
down upon the floor.

'I was that baby, and I've been looking for my mother.
I have reason to believe that…that you are her.'

Elizabeth glanced at her then, her cheeks flushed, her
eyes glazed with tears. 'You're Louise?'

Lula nodded, a lump in her own throat.

'My baby?'

She couldn't help it. Tears began. 'I am.'

'Oh…!'

Elizabeth stood up and pulled Lula into her arms,
squeezing her tight against her, but then, sensing that Lula
felt uncomfortable, she let her go. She stared at her instead,
taking her in. Every tiny inch. Then she turned and began
to pace the room, sniffing and clearing her throat, then
stopping to look at her and pace some more, before she sat
down again, suddenly stilled.

'I've thought of you *every day*.'

'What happened?' Lula looked at her through tear-
glazed eyes. 'What made you leave me on the beach?'

Elizabeth got up once again, but this time settled down
on the couch next to Lula. Tentatively she reached out and
took Lula's hand in her own, gulping as she did so.

'So many things…so many hurtful things… I've hoped
for this day for so long!'

Lula squeezed her fingers back and glanced at Olly, who
was smiling at the pair of them. He indicated that he would
step outside and leave them alone.

She appreciated his gesture. She and Elizabeth had a
lot to talk about.

* * *

As Olly stood in the cluttered kitchen, trying to hunt down some clean mugs to use for some tea, he couldn't help but stand for a moment and imagine how Lula must currently be feeling.

She had to be overjoyed. Didn't she? As well as sad that she'd found her mother but had lost so much time with her? That circumstances had split them apart?

Would circumstances split Lula and himself? She'd made no commitment to stay.

Despite his strong feelings for her, he couldn't help but compare her to Rachel. Not physically. They were nothing alike. Rachel had been the conservative-looking woman of his 'list', and he'd imposed his own expectations on her. She'd turned out to be nothing like the woman he'd expected her to be.

Lula was nothing like the woman on his list. She had some of those qualities he craved, but she was right. He wanted marriage in his future, and children at some point. Lula couldn't give him that. Nor would she commit to him. She'd said so.

But commitment was what he wanted. Love was what he needed. There didn't have to be children. Not right away. And there were things they could do these days…it might still be possible…

Olly sighed. Was he trying to persuade himself or Lula?

He slammed the kettle down and leaned against the kitchen counter, his head hanging low.

Why couldn't she be perfect?

Lula could be perfect. She'd come into his world and completely turned it upside down and he loved it! Loved *her*.

He looked up and through the dirty kitchen window, out into the garden beyond. There were large runs out there and he could see foxes inside. Wild animals within cages and runs. They shouldn't be there. They shouldn't be caged. They needed to be free.

Like Lula.

She was the biggest free spirit he'd ever met. He couldn't snare her with his demands for love and marriage and children. She couldn't give him any of that, and look what had happened when he'd tried it with Rachel.

It had all gone pear-shaped and Rachel had left him—hating him, never wanting to see him again.

He couldn't bear the idea of that happening to him and Lula. Just thinking about it almost ripped him in two.

The milk in the fridge smelt a bit dodgy, and he had no idea if the old bag of sugar was in date. Elizabeth Love needed to look after herself a bit better. The animals she cared for lived in better conditions than she did.

But perhaps she'd left herself in limbo after she'd had to give Lula away?

He could only imagine how it might feel to give her up…

It turned out that Lula's mother had fallen in love with an older boy whom she'd idolised. This boy, however, sensing her naivety, had slept with her and then discarded her when he'd got what he wanted. He'd then made sure everyone knew how *easy* Elizabeth had been. A few months later she'd discovered she was pregnant—just as she'd started college.

Unable to tell her parents, she'd hidden the pregnancy and given birth alone, then taken a bus to the seaside. Seeing a family that looked kind and caring, she'd left Lula in their beach hut and got back on the bus with a broken heart.

Hurt and betrayed, she had retreated into her own shell. Learning that it was easier to deal with animals rather than people, she had taken a course in veterinary nursing and, as soon as she'd been able to afford it, had moved out of her parents' home and started the animal rescue centre.

For all her adult life she'd looked after recovering birds, or hedgehogs, or kittens, or whatever was brought to her door, dumped and abandoned, shunning people. She'd lived this way, adopting and caring for strays and injured wildlife. And every day she'd thought of the baby she'd left behind at a beach and hoped that one day she'd find her.

'Did she look for you?' Olly asked in the car on their drive back home.

'She said she tried, but the bureaucracy and red tape were suffocating and trying to track me down through the foster system was hard. Once I'd been adopted by the Chances she lost all trace.'

Olly laid his hand on hers as she drove. 'I'm glad you've found each other.'

She nodded quickly. 'Me, too.'

The snow was turning quickly to slush, and as she drove through the lanes they could hear it splashing to the side of the road into bramble-covered ditches, revealing bright blades of grass that had been covered for too long. The sunlight glinted off the wet road and they had to shield their eyes.

When she pulled up outside Moonrose Cottage Lula did so with a big sigh.

'So what happens now?' he asked.

'How do you mean?'

'Well, you've found your mum. You've got roots now. History. A family tree. The search is over.'

'Well, just because we've found each other it doesn't mean we're suddenly going to live in each other's pockets. We'll take it slowly. Life will continue.'

He took a deep breath. 'Does this change your plans about staying in Atlee Wold? You don't *have* to be a locum, you know—you could be a permanent member of staff.' He smiled, his eyes full of hope.

She didn't want to be blunt. Nor did she want to hurt him. So she sidestepped the question. 'We'll see.'

They both got out of the car and he wandered onto the path. 'I'm going to walk back. Get some exercise. I'll see you this afternoon?'

She nodded. 'Sure.'

He leaned in to kiss her then, but she closed her eyes resolutely. 'See you later.'

'Alligator…'

She smiled and watched him walk away. Then the smile slowly disappeared from her face until she was frowning.

It had been a morning of ups and downs. She was thrilled to have finally found her mother, but had Olly read more into their relationship? *Had* he?

Perhaps I need to be more clear with him about where this is going?

Inside the cottage, she flipped open her computer and began to look for locum posts. Away from Atlee Wold. Away from Olly. Before he got too attached.

CHAPTER EIGHT

FOR A FEW WEEKS they were busy at the surgery. The winter weather had set off a string of appointments and everyone, it seemed, had a chest infection.

Lula had begun working on her own and she enjoyed the freedom it gave her to get to know the patients herself, without Olly there. But they went out on house calls together, so that Lula could learn her way around and get to know some of those who couldn't make it into the surgery, either due to ill health or the fact that they had no transport and lived on the outskirts of the village.

Patrick and Olly invited her over for a meal occasionally, and they had a few enjoyable evenings together. One night Patrick had fallen asleep in his chair and she and Olly had spent a lovely hour talking quietly in front of the fire, playing cards and, yes, she had to admit it: they'd held hands and kissed.

The next morning she had reprimanded herself.

I shouldn't be encouraging him!

But it was hard. Olly was just so...*so right for her!* And that was hard to resist when you were a young single woman, despite what she kept telling herself.

Would it matter if I let this develop?

Yes, she told herself, *it would*. It was known in the village that Olly was in the market for a possible future wife. He'd look at all relationships for their long-term value.

That wasn't what Lula was there for. Whatever they had between them, it had to be short-term fun only—no strings, no obligations.

Which would hurt him. And she didn't want to do that. Lula liked him much too much to want to hurt him.

She'd tried keeping her distance from Olly, but it was difficult. He'd become such a close friend to her, and it was hard to resist his charming smile and his loving arms. There were a few more nights that she spent in his bed, and each time she found herself craving more and more of him. She hated herself every time she tore away from his embrace to go back to Moonrose.

Olly made their relationship seem so easy. But on her own she was troubled by how involved she was becoming, knowing she would have to break his heart.

The one thing I said I wouldn't do!

Why did she keep returning to his bed? To his arms? Every time she did it she'd go back to Moonrose berating herself, telling herself that it was absolutely the last time she would do it!

But it never stayed that way. She couldn't keep her distance from him—it was too hard.

Each time she attempted to create distance Olly just closed the gap more and more. And as the date came nearer for his father's retirement from the practice she found herself locked away with Olly, planning Patrick's surprise retirement party. Planning that quickly turned into handholding, then kissing, and then, before she knew what was happening, passionate lovemaking.

She was like a little bumble bee, and Olly was her pollen. The golden dust that she needed to survive.

Each time she went home she took a little piece of him in her heart. Each time she sat alone in her cottage, rats on her shoulder and Anubis in the palm of her hand, she would tell herself not to do it any more. Not to care for Olly as deeply as she did.

Not to…love him?

Did she love him? She hoped not. She'd not come to Atlee Wold to fall in love. She'd not come to have her heart broken, or to break someone else's.

The tarantula breakthrough had happened after she'd met her mother. She'd gone home, drunk a large glass of wine and then braved it. Putting her whole hand into the tank. Lula had been scared, but the terror had gone. She'd gained strength from her meeting with Elizabeth. As Anubis had tentatively stepped onto the palm of her hand with his long, hairy, surprisingly solid legs, she'd almost stopped breathing. But then she'd taken a deep breath, acknowledged the heavy spider on her palm and then begun breathing again.

Olly had been so proud of her when she'd told him. After all, it had been one of her greatest fears and challenges to herself and she'd overcome it.

All she had to do now was tell Olly that she would be leaving in a month's time and then create another challenge for herself. Something to do with heights? They'd always scared her, hadn't they? And if dependable Olly could do it, with his parachute jump…

She'd found another locum post. In Portsmouth—the place of her abandonment. It had seemed the perfect place to go to. To come full circle and visit the beach she'd been found on. The post would start one week after she'd left Atlee Wold. That should give her enough time to return Anubis to his rightful owner, unpack her belongings and choose some new challenges for herself.

The new post was on the coast, close to where she'd originally been left as a baby, and she wondered about all the things she hadn't tried—windsurfing, kitesurfing, jet-skiing, scuba-diving. A whole host of challenges she could set herself. Maybe a bungee jump for charity?

The post wouldn't be too far away from her mother. She could still visit her—maybe once a month. Although at the moment she was visiting Elizabeth a couple of times a week.

They'd shared quite a bit, and Elizabeth had shown Lula all the newspaper cuttings about her case that she kept in an old scrapbook, faded with time.

Getting to know her mother had been something Lula had imagined often, but the real thing far surpassed her dreams. They were similar in many ways—in their character, and in the way they thought about life and politics, and in the television programmes they both watched. Their shared love for animals was amazing. As Elizabeth taught Lula about the ways of foxes, and how to keep a baby bird alive, Lula told her mother about Nefertiti and Cleo and the exotic Anubis.

Elizabeth had gained something from their reunion, too. Each time Lula returned another part of her house had been cleared out and cleaned. It was as though Elizabeth was finally reclaiming her life from the dirt and the dust and the random objects that held a connection to the past.

Elizabeth had been upset to hear about her daughter's fight against leukaemia, and had been in tears as Lula told her about her years of struggle. She'd learnt about other members of her family who were still alive. Elizabeth's parents were both dead, but Elizabeth had two brothers. They were all going to meet up at some point, and she'd spoken to them on the phone about Lula. One had even cried, and she'd been touched by the way she was being received by everyone.

Being received by her family would be easier than saying goodbye.

She'd already told Elizabeth—just not Olly. Or his father.

And they'd want to know. They'd need to know that they had to find another doctor to take her place.

I have to tell him now.

Lula rapped on his door. The spring sunshine was shining brightly. All the snow had gone and daffodils were blooming, showing their golden trumpets throughout the village.

When Olly opened the door he caught her biting her lip. 'Why are you knocking? I told you before—come straight in.'

He stepped back so she could follow him inside. They went into the kitchen, where his father sat reading a newspaper at the table.

Patrick peered at her over his glasses. 'Lula! How lovely to see you. How is our favourite locum? Thinking of becoming a permanent partner, I hope?'

He beamed a smile at her and Lula wished the floor would swallow her up whole. It wasn't just going to be Olly who would be upset at her plans.

'Actually, that's why I'm here. I've come to a decision.'

'Brilliant,' Olly said, sitting down at the table and pulling out a chair for her to sit down, too. 'Dad and I have been discussing it for some time—about how well you fit in and how everyone loves you.'

I do hope you *don't love me, Olly.*

Though she knew the truth in her heart. It was obvious he had strong feelings for her—even though he knew she couldn't give him what he wanted. It was in the way he was with her…the way she caught him looking at her when he thought she wouldn't notice. The way he acted…the way he thought of her. The way he held her in his arms. The way he made love to her.

All the things she'd tried to avoid.

'Thank you. I have loved it here, but… The time has come for me to move on. To take up a new post.' She hurried on, seeing the smiles drop from their faces. 'I've found a new post—a locum post like this one—down in Portsmouth. I think it could be perfect for me.'

Olly stared at her, his eyes darkening with disappointment and anger. 'You're…leaving?'

She licked her lips. 'I'm sorry. Maybe I should have told you earlier. But there's been so much stuff going on with Elizabeth and myself that I let it slide. I apologise for that.'

'But…your *mother*'s here—and the *practice* is here— and patients that adore you.'

'And I'll miss them, Olly, but it was never my intention to stay. Even if I did find my mother.'

'But—'

His father interrupted him, laying a firm hand on his son's arm. 'It's Lula's choice, son. We can't force her.' He turned to Lula. 'I can't say I'm not disappointed. I really think you're an amazing person, and I for one would have loved it if you'd stayed permanently. Part of me was hoping that you and Olly would run the practice as partners.' He coloured. 'In more ways than one, if you catch my meaning. I know you two have grown close.'

Tears began to sting her eyes. She liked Patrick a lot. It hurt to know she was disappointing him, but she had to stick to her plan and leave. If she stayed she and Olly would no doubt become even closer and their relationship would deepen. Then he would want to have children. She knew he would. He'd told her he wanted kids. He was traditional that way.

But she couldn't give him that. She was infertile. She would never be able to have children and that would tear them apart. She'd seen it happen to so many couples. She wasn't going to put herself through it. Nor him. She loved him too much for that.

'I'm so sorry, Patrick. I know it's not what you wanted

to hear.' She stood up and went to leave, but Olly grabbed her wrist.

'Wait!'

She turned, determined not to let the tears fall. 'Yes, Olly?'

'I can't lose you.'

A brave smile made her face even sadder. 'Yes, you can. And it's best we do it now. Before it hurts us all too much.'

She pulled her hand free and hurried from his house, slamming the door shut behind her. She burst into tears as she ran down the pathway and into Betsy.

After all her efforts not to get hurt, here she was, crying over leaving him. Leaving Atlee Wold. Leaving Patrick. Leaving her beloved patients whom she'd got to know. Leaving her mother—though they'd still visit each other. Portsmouth wasn't that far away…

She stuck her key into the ignition, cleared her eyes and drove away.

Olly stared in disbelief at the closed door. Lula was leaving? But…she *couldn't*! She was…perfect. She was… They'd been getting so close he'd assumed she'd stay—especially now that she knew her mother was here!

He took a step forward, as if to go after her, but something stopped him. He turned, sadness making his heart feel heavy, and looked at his father. 'I can't believe she won't stay.'

'No, but we always knew this was a possibility.'

'I can't lose her, Dad.'

'You have to let her go. You can't force her to stay. Look at what happened with Rachel.'

'Rachel was different! Rachel was wrong for me! Right from the start. I was trying to force a square peg into a round hole. She was a city girl—a medical rep. A party girl. I knew she wasn't right for me, but I tried to make her fit in with my life. To force her to enjoy quiet village life. I might as well have asked her to arrange the church flowers as something to do!'

'And Lula? *She's* not your run-of-the-mill girl.'

'No, she isn't. She's amazing. Sweet and loving and… We fit, Dad. We *fit*!'

'But you have the same problem, son. You can't force her to stay.'

'It wouldn't be force. She loves it here—I know she does. She loves the people, the practice, the ladies in her dance class. She loves the serenity here.'

'Does she love *you*?'

Olly looked at his father. He thought she did.

He hoped she did.

Because it was the only way he could make her stay.

Mrs Broadstairs had just left Lula's room and she was about to call in her last patient when Olly came in, closing the door firmly behind him. She could see he had something to say as he paced about before her desk.

It was her last day at the surgery. One patient to go. The atmosphere between herself and Olly had been functional, not frosty, since her announcement. He'd made no effort to go out of his way to see her and she had done the same with him. It was easier that way—the less they saw of each other the better.

But now he was here, standing tall and defiantly masculine in her room, opposite her desk. His sheer presence made her realise how much she'd missed him. Missed his touch. His arms around her. His lips upon her skin. His gentle kisses all over her body…

'Yes?' She hoped her voice sounded solid and unaffected.

His jaw was clenching and unclenching; his hands were upon his hips. 'I had to come and see you.'

She didn't say anything.

'I can't say I agree with your choice, but I don't want you to think I don't care. I…er…I'm here to offer to help you pack. That way I can put my grandmother's things into storage at the same time. We're putting the cottage up for sale.'

Oh. She hadn't expected that. She'd thought Moonrose Cottage would always be a part of the James family.

'There's no need.'

'There's every need. I need to catalogue everything, and I might as well do it whilst helping you pack. Make sure you don't leave anything behind.'

Lula nodded. 'Right. Well, there's not much left to do, but okay. If you want to help I've a few boxes I need to fill.'

'When's the removal lorry coming?'

'Around ten o'clock. But it's just a small one. I haven't got much to take with me.'

Olly clenched his jaw some more and she could tell he was fighting the urge to say something else to her. She would have given anything to run her fingers along his jawline, to soften his anger and release his tension.

But that wouldn't be a good idea.

It was best not to touch him. To remind herself of what he felt like. Though she could recall it quite easily. He was imprinted in her memory for evermore.

'Have you found someone yet?' she asked.

Olly frowned, his face like thunder. 'What do you mean?'

'Another locum. Someone to take my place.'

He stared hard at her, his brow creased with lines she'd never seen before, his eyes like the depths of a dark ocean. 'I could never find someone to take your place.'

And he turned in an instant, slamming the door as he left.

Lula stared at the spot he'd stood in, her breathing laboured, realising how much her leaving was upsetting him.

Well, it would hurt you a lot more further down the road, Olly. It might not feel like it now, but I'm doing the best thing for us.

I am.

Olly stood outside her surgery door and let out a pent-up breath. He was trying to use reverse psychology. By offering to help her pack, by offering to make sure she packed properly, he hoped she'd realise all the things she'd miss if she went away. He wanted her last thoughts of the village to be filled with him and his presence, and he knew that by being with her he'd be able to talk to her some more, try and persuade her otherwise if there was a chance that she'd show him she loved him.

Because wasn't love all that really mattered?

Wasn't love the most important thing? The thing that made the world turn? That made people find the strength to get up each day and face life?

He wasn't going to force Lula to do anything. She had to stay of her own volition, but he wanted a choice. Options. When Rachel had left he hadn't been given a choice in anything. She'd made all the decisions. She'd decided on an abortion. She decided to leave without telling him. He'd never been given the courtesy of choice.

Well, he'd like it now, thank you very much.

It was the morning of moving day. Lula was dressed in old jeans and a green-and-black-checked lumberjack shirt that she usually did painting in. Her hair was tied back with a blue bandana, except for the long fringe of pink and purple hair that fell over the left side of her face.

Packing was hard work. She really hadn't thought she had much, but she was finding her belongings all over the cottage.

Anubis was still plugged in to the wall, with electricity

powering the small lamp in the top of his tank, but she was hoping to drop him off at her friend's place on her way to Portsmouth. The rats had a blanket over their cage and were also ready to go, though she could see they'd managed to pull some of the blanket through the bars and chew on it.

A feeling of hurt filled her when she stood at the kitchen window and looked out upon the long back garden. A garden that was beginning to fill with bloom and blossom. A garden whose roses she would never see in full bloom. A garden that had once housed a scared teenager in its shed. A teenager who was now back home and being a mother to her baby with the support of her family.

So much had happened since Lula had come to Atlee Wold, and she knew she'd remember every part of it: Patrick, Ruby and the baby, Mrs Macabee, Bonnie, her dance class, all her patients and their families. The surgery.

Olly.

Dr Oliver James.

Possibly the most handsome man she would ever know or have the misfortune to love. A man she should never have got close to.

Just thinking about leaving him was painful. But she knew she had to do it. It was the only way to stop them both from hurting even more further down the line, when Olly wanted to realise his dream of having children.

She heard a bump from upstairs and wondered what he was doing. He'd arrived about an hour ago. Grey and glum, with enormous bags under his eyes that spoke volumes about a sleepless night. She'd had one herself. Going over it all in her mind.

But she was doing it for him. For *them*.

She'd come back for visits. Her mother was in Atlee Wold—that would always be true for as long as Elizabeth was alive. Every month or so she'd return. It wasn't a proper goodbye, after which they'd never see each other again. It wasn't as if she was deserting him, was it?

Another thud, and this time she heard him swear before he came thundering down the stairs and rushing over to the sink, holding his thumb under the cold tap.

'Are you okay?'

'Caught my hand on a nail.'

There was plenty of blood, and Lula ripped open one of her boxes and pulled out a first-aid kit, rummaging for bandages and scissors and tape. 'Let me see.'

'I'm all right, Lula.'

'Let me see—'

'I said I'm all *right*!' he shouted at her, and she stood back from him, shocked. He'd never, ever raised his voice at her like that and she wasn't used to it.

The shock on her face must have been clear, because he sighed and then apologised. 'I'm sorry. I didn't mean to shout.'

'I'm just trying to help,' she said quietly.

'I know. I'm just…frustrated, that's all.'

'With me?' She stood at his side, a whole head shorter than him.

'Who else would drive me to distraction?'

He grimaced and pulled his thumb free of the water. But the blood still seeped out and he had to push it back under the flow again.

She opened a gauze pad and then grabbed his hand, pulling it towards her and wrapping the pad tightly around his thumb.

'This might need stitches.' She held it firmly, then indicated that he should do so as she wound a bandage around his thumb.

By the time she was done his hand looked comical with its big bandage and he couldn't help but smile. 'Thanks.'

'No problem. Get someone to take you to A&E. That needs stitches.'

'Dad'll do it.'

'You need the proper equipment.'

'We have it at the surgery. We used to perform minor ops there—don't worry about it.' He got up and moved away from her.

Lula could still feel the way his cold hand had felt in hers. His hands were so large compared to her dainty ones, but they had fitted so well together. She had spent hours one bedtime, lying there, examining his hands and looking at the way they interlocked with hers...

There was the toot of a horn from outside. She got up to walk to the front of the cottage. 'The lorry's here.'

'Right. Marvellous.'

'It shouldn't take them more than an hour to pack up my stuff...maybe half that.'

'And then you'll go?'

She nodded. Had his voice cracked on that last word? 'I'm sorry this hurts you, Olly. I can't say it enough, but it's the right thing to do.'

He shook his head. 'For who?'

'For us. You know this, Olly. You *know* it! You're a traditional guy. You want the whole relationship, marriage and kids package—you know you do! I can't give you that!'

He stalked across the room and took her hands in his. 'But I *love* you, Lula! Surely that counts for something?'

How could he do this to her? Today? 'Of course it does... and I love you, too. Yes, I do. I know you think I don't, and that I'm heartless and just walking away, but I'm not! I'm protecting us. I'm protecting *you*!'

'From what? I'm a big boy, Lula, I can look after myself.'

'From *me*. Believe me, you don't want the hurt that I'll cause you some day, when it finally sinks in that I can't have the babies you want.'

'I want to be with *you*. Babies is something for the future—I'm not thinking about that right now.'

'Well I am. Because I have to!' She pulled free and began stacking her boxes by the front door, slamming them down on top of each other, determined not to let him see her crying.

'You never even gave us a chance.'

'How dare you? Of course I did. We had fun, didn't we? We had our time together? Was that not giving us a chance?'

'You always intended to walk away, but you never bothered to tell me that.'

'I didn't think I had to. I was a locum. The word itself implies being temporary. I thought my life was my own.'

'It is. But then you slept with me, and we got involved and started going out. Forgive me if I'm wrong, but I thought if you were in a relationship with someone then you told them your intentions!'

She slammed another box down on the floor, its contents rattling dangerously. 'Did you tell me yours?'

'What?' He looked puzzled.

'Did you ever tell me *your* intentions?'

'Well…no. But we were in a relationship together, I thought we were moving forward. I thought we were together…'

'You *thought*… You never asked me once what I might think. Did you?'

'Because I thought you were telling me everything already. By being with me. I thought you were declaring your intention to stay.'

'You assumed—and you know what assumptions make…' She yanked open the front door and indicated the stack of boxes to the two removal guys.

Olly followed her into the blossoming front garden. The Blue Moon roses the cottage was named for had not yet bloomed. 'Aren't *you* assuming? Assuming that I'll want kids?'

'Don't you?'

He ground his teeth. 'Yes. But there are ways around that—ways to fight infertility. You should know that better than anyone. You *are* a doctor.'

'Yes, I am! Don't you see that's the reason? Olly? Don't you *see*?' She began to cry. Nothing could stop the tears from flowing. Nothing could stop this dam from opening. For now he'd got to the root of the problem that had bothered her for years. 'Don't you know why I fill my life to the brim and constantly challenge myself?'

He shook his head.

'Because I'm the *same* as you. I *am*. I'm a traditionalist, too. I want marriage and, dammit, yes, *I want children*. And I want to have them with you most of all. But I know I can't. I'm leaving now to protect *myself*—not just you. I have to leave because I can't bear to be with you and not be able to give you the one thing that I want most for myself!'

She leaned back against the garden gate, her arms folded over her chest as she sobbed.

'The hair, the rats, the dancing—all the crazy things that make me *me* are crazy things that keep my mind off the one thing I want most in the world. I have to leave, Olly. It would be *torture* to stay and see your face when every month nothing happens.'

She turned her back on him and walked into the cottage.

Olly stood there, shell-shocked, digesting her words. Wasn't there *anything* he could do to change this? He stood in the garden unmoving, like a statue. The removal men walked back and forth past him, loading up Lula's boxes. The urge to get them from the lorry and put them back in the cottage was stronger than anything he'd ever experienced before.

How could he make her change her mind? He'd told her

he loved her and it was true. He'd fallen in love with Dr Lula Chance. Lula Love. Louise. Whatever name she chose to go by. He didn't care about the crazy things that made her who she was. He *loved* those crazy things! He loved *her*! Lula! All five foot three of her. And he couldn't imagine his life without her in it!

Olly darted back into the house to try and persuade her to stay, to give them both a chance, but she was standing there, holding her rat cage, her handbag over her shoulder. Anubis was already gone. Packed safely in the lorry. He had to let her know that she was more than just a breeding machine. That her inability to have kids wasn't what defined her.

It all looked so final now.

'Don't go. Please.'

'Olly, don't do this…'

'I'm begging you. I will get down on my knees if you want—but, Lula, you can't go.'

'I have to.'

'Lula—'

She pushed past him. '*No*, Olly!'

She hurried down the path towards Betsy, placing the rat cage carefully in the back, then moved round to the driver's door.

Olly ran to her side and held the car door, preventing her from shutting it. 'You can't leave like this! I *love* you—does that not count for anything?'

There were tears all down her face, and her eyes were reddened and swollen from crying. 'Oh, it counts.'

But she wouldn't be stopped. She was determined to go and she pulled the door shut and started the engine.

Olly stepped back, contemplating throwing himself onto the bonnet of her car. He didn't care who saw. All he could think was that the woman he loved was about to drive out of his life because she couldn't give him children.

He banged on the window. 'I don't need to have children. I just need *you*!'

She shook her head sadly and then turned away.

He heard her shift the car into first gear and then the Beetle called Betsy carried his beloved Lula away down the lane. He watched her go, hoping that the car would stop, that she'd turn around, get out, come running back—anything… But she didn't do any of those things.

Betsy and Lula disappeared.

Olly sank to his knees in the street, tears on his face, oblivious to all who were watching.

CHAPTER NINE

OLLY STARED AT his computer. There were a patient's details up on the screen: name, address, date of birth and medical history. The patient herself was even sitting in front of him, talking about something or other, but he wasn't really listening.

Lula had been gone for four weeks. Four interminably long weeks in which his father had decided against early retirement and had promised to stay on at the practice until they found a suitable long-term replacement.

No more locums, he'd said. Unless they got desperate.

Olly was past desperate. He was forlorn and lost. The first few days after she'd gone he'd kept himself optimistic with the thought that she'd come back. That she'd realise her mistake, discover she couldn't live without him and return.

He'd believed it so much he'd even kept the cottage clean and the fire ready in case she needed it. But as those first few days had turned into a week, and then two, he'd stopped going to the cottage and had accepted that she wasn't coming back. Lula was well and truly gone.

He'd lost her. The one woman he'd ever truly loved.

He kept checking his phones, his landline and mobile, to see if there were any texts or messages, but both phones were stubbornly silent and devoid of anything from Lula. He wasn't eating properly and seemed to exist on tea. Once he'd even gone round to Elizabeth Love's house and sat and talked to her, but even though Lula had been in contact with her mother she hadn't mentioned Olly at all.

He knew she'd started her post in Portsmouth and had thought about writing to her, but each time he took up a pen and paper or clicked on his emails, the words wouldn't come.

What could he say that he hadn't already said?

His patient was still talking.

'…and then he said he wouldn't take in my papers or mail or feed the cat because he had a life of his own, and that I'd have to find someone else to do it. I mean, does that sound like a kindly neighbour to you?'

He registered the last part. Mrs Bates was always in, complaining about her neighbour Mr Brown. Olly somewhat suspected there might be something between them, or maybe there once had been, because they certainly seemed to bicker about each other a lot.

'I don't know what to say, Mrs Bates. Mr Brown does like to keep himself to himself.'

'But that's not normal, is it? Neighbours aren't like what they used to be.' She tutted in a haughty manner. 'People used to look out for each other in my day. Help one another. Like that lady doctor that used to be here…Dr Chance. She helped me out whenever I asked, and she even gave me extra tuition at her dancing class. And she wasn't a neighbour. Just a friend, really. But she helped out.' Mrs Bates settled her hands on her lap, clutching the strap of her handbag. 'She was a lovely doctor—it's a pity she didn't stay.'

Olly swallowed hard, but the lump in his throat wouldn't budge. 'She was.'

'Such a pretty thing, too. Single, she said. I thought you and she might become an item…'

Mrs Bates was fishing. She knew full well that he and Lula had been seeing each other—she just wanted confirmation from the horse's mouth.

He stared at a pile of paperwork. 'She had to move on.'

'But not before she found her family—isn't that right, Doctor? Lizzy Love confirmed it herself—told me that Dr Chance was her long-lost daughter!'

He nodded. 'I believe so.'

'You'd think she'd stay. You know…for family.'

But it had never just been about family. Had it? Lula had come to find her mother, yes, but had got involved with Olly, too. And even though she wanted children—badly, as it turned out—she'd walked away from trying to find out if she could have them with him.

He'd lied about possibly not wanting children. Of *course* he wanted kids. His own parents had been great. His dad had told him about his mum—about how wonderful she'd been and all those cute stories about her. He'd had a good childhood even with just his father to look after him. He wanted to be a father himself, it was true. He was a traditionalist.

But Lula's leukaemia had made her infertile. Or rather the chemo had. And she believed that he would hate her eventually for not being able to give him the children he so badly wanted.

I could never have hated her. We would have found a way. I'm sure of it!

Medical technology was moving on all the time. Miracles happened. And if they didn't for them then there were other options—surrogacy, adoption, fostering, IVF. Solutions that other people used but Lula was not willing to contemplate.

Perhaps the urge to have a child was stronger for her than he'd realised?

Mrs Bates realised she wasn't going to get anything out of him gossip-wise and stood and saw herself out. After she'd gone he let out a big sigh and leaned back in his chair, his head in his hands.

No more patients today. His afternoon was free.

If he went back to the house he'd just rattle around the rooms until bedtime, and it was difficult being at home. So many of the rooms contained memories of Lula. Especially his bedroom, where they'd shared themselves physically. He hated climbing into bed alone, without her. He hated waking up alone just to go through another day of tormenting himself.

I'll go and see Lula's mother again.

She might have heard more from Lula.

Elizabeth Love was out feeding her chickens, spreading seed across the grass as the brown fluffy birds pecked and scratched at the ground, their heads bobbing back and forth, cackling away.

Olly got out of his car and waved a hand in greeting.

'Oliver! I haven't seen you for a week—have you been all right?'

'Existing. Still breathing. Does that count?'

'I miss her, too. But I guess I've had years of experience, so I can cope with it better.'

He smiled. It had been her choice. To give up Lula. He couldn't forget that. Though he understood her reasons.

'It is hard…' He leaned against her broken gate, and then pushed away from it forcefully. 'There just doesn't seem to be any point to anything now!'

Elizabeth blinked at him. The sun was in her eyes. 'Of course there's a point.'

'I can't see it if it's there. Life just seems so…*flat*… without her in it.'

She came over to him and laid a hand on his arm. 'Oliver…sometimes it's darkest before dawn.'

'Are you saying everything will be better in the morning? Because my dad's been saying that for nearly a month now, and let me tell you the mornings are the worst.'

'Why?'

'Because she's not *there*. Her head isn't on my pillow… her body isn't beside me. I can't hear her laughter or see her smile or…' he laughed wryly '…watch her dancing in her belly-dancing class.'

'I don't know what to say. She made a choice. I can't judge her. Not after what I did.' She picked up a watering can and began to water her flowerpots.

'It was the wrong choice.'

'Not for her. Have you gone after her? Tried to persuade her to come back?'

He shook his head and waved away an annoying fly. 'I don't have her address.'

'I do.' Elizabeth smiled.

He looked up. 'You do?' Hope began to build.

'It's in the house. She sent it to me yesterday and made me promise not to give it to you.'

He frowned. 'But you will, right? Otherwise you wouldn't have told me about it, and if you held it back now that would be outright mental cruelty.'

'I'll give it to you—but only because I can see how much she means to you and I saw what you were like together. You were good. You were right. Wait here.'

She disappeared into her house and came out after a minute or so, clutching a piece of paper. She passed it to him.

'I never gave it to you. You sneaked a look whilst I was making some tea, all right?'

He opened the paper, read the address, and then beamed a smile at her before leaning forward and kissing her cheek. 'You're a star.'

He could go and find her!

She laughed. 'I'm a romantic. Go get her. *Tell* her. Make her *believe*.'

He nodded and raced back to his car, gunning the engine.

* * *

The drive to Portsmouth seemed to take forever. It should have been no more than an hour's drive, but he got stuck behind a tractor on his way out of Atlee Wold, and then in a traffic jam on the A3. There'd been an accident. He'd been torn between staying in his car and remaining patient, or gnawing at his wrists to take his mind off his frustration! Once he got past the accident—an empty horse box had overturned—it was a straight drive down to the Solent.

He passed through the Hindhead Tunnel and drove through the hills of Petersfield. When he saw the first sign for the coastal town of Portsmouth his stomach began to churn with nerves.

He had no idea what he was going to say to her. What could he say that he hadn't told her already? But she *had* to see—especially after his drive down to seek her out—just how much she meant to him.

His heart was racing with excitement at the idea of seeing her again. There'd been a palpable ache in his chest for weeks, and now that he knew he might see her again that weight had lifted and he felt he could breathe again.

Olly knew he had to persuade her somehow. And it felt so good to know that he was going to see her again! Her smile...her face...the wonderful colours in her hair... Hear her laughter... He'd missed her so much!

As he drove ever closer to Portsmouth, where Lula's story had begun, he began to feel his nerves drumming in his tight stomach. He looked across the water and saw all the boats resting at anchor. He thought how peaceful it all looked. Then, before he knew it, he was driving into the city, passing the big white sails, listening to his satnav as it guided him through the housing areas of Southsea. In the distance he could see, rising above everything else, a pure white tower that stretched up into the blue sky. The

Spinnaker Tower. He'd heard of it. There was something similar in Dubai.

He couldn't help but wonder what kind of life she'd made for herself here. He could see its attraction. Its charm. The Isle of Wight was across the water…there was its length of beach. There was even a funfair, like the kind he'd visited as a child.

He drove on, looking for Dickens Way, and suddenly there it was. He hit the brakes and made a right-hand turn into the street, looking for her house. It was a long street, narrow, and packed with terraced houses that all looked quite similar. The road was jam-packed with cars, bumper to bumper on either side.

Gritting his teeth, and muttering curses at there being nowhere to park, he had to drive further away to find a side road, squeeze into a space and then hurry back. He was sweating and anxious and fidgety. His mind was racing. What would she say when she saw him? Would she be pleased? He was assuming she would be. But what if she wasn't? What if she thought this was an embarrassing errand? What if he'd misread her feelings for him?

No. She told me she loved me!

He wiped his brow, straightening his crooked tie and tucking in his shirt.

He let out a deep breath, squared his shoulders and walked up the path. He was a bag of nerves. His legs were like wobbly blancmange, no strength to them at all, and his stomach was churning and tumbling as if he was on a fairground ride. He wished he'd brought some water. Or something stronger. Like beer. Or a straight shot of vodka.

Something.

He was just seconds away from meeting her…seeing her…

Olly rapped his knuckles on the red door. Then, just for good measure, he rang the doorbell, too, hearing a deep gong noise inside. He waited and he waited. Then he waited some more.

What was going on? Where was she?

Perhaps she was at work? He decided to have a look through the downstairs window, but couldn't see anything through the net curtains.

He blocked the sun with his hands to peer in, but it didn't help at all.

What was he to do?

The surgery. The doctors' surgery. They'd know, surely?

But he didn't know where that was. He quickly stepped over a low brick wall and rapped on the door of the house next to Lula's. He heard some shouting inside, and a child crying.

A woman answered the door. 'Yes?'

'Hi—could you tell me where the local doctors' surgery is, please?'

'Oh, I thought you were going to try and sell me something. Right—it's a couple of streets over, in St Thomas' Avenue.' She leaned out to point. 'Down this road, take a left, go about a hundred yards and then it's on your right.'

'St Thomas' Avenue? Thank you.'

The woman nodded and closed the door.

He didn't bother going back for his car. He figured it would be easier to walk. Besides, he had no idea if he'd be able to get a parking space anywhere near!

His churning stomach was now mixing nervous energy with frustration. This wasn't the way he'd planned it! He'd expected to find her at the house. With the house empty, he was beginning to feel a little irritated.

It wasn't going as he'd wanted. He'd expected to be kissing her by now! To have surprised her and swept her off her feet, told her once again how much he loved her and asked would she come back?

The surgery was in the centre of Portsmouth, and because of the lovely hot weather he enjoyed the short walk to it, even if his mouth was as dry as the bottom of a birdcage.

The building was split into two practices, and she could have been at either one. The receptionist at the first one couldn't tell him anything, and he had to get in a queue at the next. Olly waited impatiently, tapping his feet and trying to peer round the people in front of him, sighing heavily when they took ages with their turns. When he got to the receptionist he rested against the chest-high counter and stated his request.

'I'm looking for Dr Lula Chance. I believe she may be here as a locum?'

The receptionist nodded and smiled. 'Yes, she started here—but she's left already, I'm afraid.'

'Left?' How could she have left? 'Where has she gone?'

'I'm afraid I don't know. It was very sudden.'

'Sudden? She wasn't taken ill?'

The receptionist shook her head. 'I can't give out any private details, I'm afraid.'

'I'm a doctor.'

'I'm afraid I'm not at liberty to say.'

She smiled sympathetically and Olly knew realistically that her hands were tied. Unfortunately that didn't help him.

So she'd been a no-show at the house, she'd left her job already, and no one could tell him why. Where would she have gone?

'Do you have a forwarding address?'

'I'm sorry. I can't give you that information.'

He was not a violent man, but this wasn't going the way he'd hoped. 'Of course not. Thank you.'

He was about to step away when the receptionist perked up and said, 'But I *can* tell you she's doing a sponsored abseil today.'

Olly looked up. 'A *what*?'

'A sponsored abseil. She's raising money for childhood leukaemia.'

He gripped the reception desk. 'Where?'

The receptionist smiled. 'The Spinnaker Tower. She must be crazy, if you ask me—it's over five hundred feet high!'

The tower. He'd seen it driving in to the city. She was up *there*? Of course she was! He couldn't help but smile to himself. Of *course* she was up there! She'd be challenging herself, or something, wouldn't she? Doing one of her crazy stunts.

Well, that was one tower he was quite happy to rescue a maiden from!

If she'd let him…

Olly thanked the receptionist and raced back for his car. All he had to do now was find the way to get there.

At Gunwharf Quays he went running through the crowds, pushing past, apologising for knocking into people as he passed.

The Spinnaker Tower loomed above him—a pure white needle stretching upwards into the azure-blue sky. At the top were some viewing platforms, and just below them he could see a group of dark figures—like blackfly on a rose.

The abseilers!

On the ground there was another group of people, wearing helmets and abseiling gear, grinning madly or having their photos taken.

Olly rushed over.

'Lula? *Lula?*' He looked at each of them, hoping that she was already down, that she'd done it already, that he wouldn't have to watch her do this.

But how amazing it would be for her! He knew she didn't like heights. She'd said so when he'd mentioned the

parachute jump. The one he'd not actually done because...
Well, heights weren't his thing, either!

He looked up at the tower, fearing where he might have
to go to get Lula back.

The group's leader laid a hand on his shoulder. 'Can I
help you?'

'I'm looking for Dr Lula Chance?'

The leader nodded, then pointed. 'She's up there. Last
one to come down. But she's nervous and won't budge.'

Olly looked up. Higher and higher, to the top of the
tower. 'Can I get up there?'

'In the lift—but you can't abseil. Not unless you sign
up and pay for it.'

Sign up? *Abseil?* From up *there*?

Gulping away the nausea that suddenly filled him, he
rushed into the base of the tower and grabbed a handful
of notes from his wallet to pay for his ascendance to the
top. The lift filled with sightseers—people who wanted to
go to the viewing platforms and gaze out across the naval
city—and they all seemed to take an age to file in before
the lift doors closed.

Not him, though.

Portsmouth was probably gorgeous, but the one thing
he wanted to see was Lula. Nothing else.

Eventually the door closed, and he felt his stomach drop
as the lift moved upwards. Impatiently he stood with the
tourists, waiting for them to climb to the top of the tower,
hoping that she wouldn't start her descent before he could
get to her. Hoping that her nerves would make her wait
until he got there.

Ping.

The door opened and he rushed out, heading over to the
roped-off area where he'd seen the people assembled earlier. There was a young guy there, with a ring piercing his
nose, wearing abseiling gear and a helmet.

'Lula Chance? Where is she? I need to talk to her!' He grabbed the man's arm to make him look at him.

The young lad pointed through a door. 'She's in there, mate. About to descend. But you can't go through.'

'I need to speak to her. It's urgent!'

'I can't let you go through. Abseilers only, I'm afraid. The outer doors are open, and without safety equipment—'

'Then kit me up! Look.' He pulled his wallet from his back pocket. 'I'll pay the registration fee.'

'I dunno, mate…'

'Do you want to raise money for leukaemia or not? I'll sign one of those waivers—whatever—but I need to go through!'

The nose-ring lad seemed to think about it for a moment, then nodded and pulled a piece of paper from the desk behind him. 'Here you go.'

'Thanks!' Olly scribbled his signature on the form and then jumped over the rope and pushed past him, yanking open the door.

'*Lula!*'

He found himself in a corridor, with narrow stairs leading down to an open door through which a strong gust of warm wind was blowing. Outside there was a narrow platform, with a couple of people on it. One on the platform and the other climbing over. He saw wisps of purple hair…

'Lula! Wait!'

There was real fear in her eyes, and she was gripping onto the arms of the guide for dear life, but she heard him call out and looked up.

'Olly?'

Her eyes met his and it was like a thousand lightning bolts smacking him in the guts. There she was. Looking as wonderful and as gorgeous as he'd ever seen her! And she was standing on a really narrow ledge with a massive drop behind her…

The guide took one look at him and held up a hand. 'Stay back! You can't come out here!'

He held up his hands. 'I'm abseiling, too.'

'Not without kit, you're not!'

Olly looked about him and saw an organised puddle of belts and metal clips arranged on the floor. He'd seen people do this, so he stepped into one of the harnesses and pulled it up over his trousers, tightening it about his waist.

'Better?'

'Look…she's about to descend a hundred metres, mate. I think she needs to concentrate on what she's doing, don't you?'

'I need to speak to her.'

'You'll have to do it at the bottom.' He grabbed his walkie-talkie and spoke into it.

Olly gazed at Lula. 'Lula…I love you. I need you.'

She smiled, her eyes brimming with tears. Then she nodded. 'I love you, too.'

'We can be together!' he shouted, hoping she could hear in his voice how much he meant it.

She stared at him. 'Olly, I'm scared.'

'You? You're the bravest woman I know.'

'I don't feel brave right now.'

'You can do anything you put your mind to. I need to be with you, Lula. I'm not going away.'

She locked eyes with him, then nodded. 'Watch me. Will you do that? I'll be able to do this if you're watching me.'

He nodded. 'I'll watch every step.'

Unbelievably, he saw her let go and his heart froze. She was going to go! She was going to do it! He couldn't help but see the map of the city spread out beneath her, and all he could think about was the drop.

The guy who was guiding the ropes from above beckoned him over. 'Let me check you're fastened correctly.'

He patted him down and tested the ropes and harness were all set up correctly. 'You signed the form?'

Olly nodded and gulped. Was he really going to do this? There was nothing *making* him do it. He could turn around. Go down in the lift. He'd still give the money to the charity—it wouldn't matter if he backed out. What was a few hundred metres between strangers?

The guide beckoned him forward. 'She's frozen.'

His heart stopped beating. She was stuck on the way down? *How?* It should be impossible to get stuck doing something like this. The only reason she wouldn't be moving would be if…

If she was scared stiff.

Lula had to be scared. Terrified. Frozen to the side of the tower. He knew he had to help her.

'Let me go down, too. I'll talk her through it.'

The guy shook his head. 'All right, mate. But you'll follow my exact instructions, yes?'

'Absolutely.'

He ran through the instructions and Olly fastened on his helmet and clipped himself onto the rope. The guide made sure he was securely tethered, and then allowed him to step over the safety barrier.

'Wish me luck?'

The guy shook his head. 'You won't need it.' He tapped him on the helmet and let go.

Olly plummeted. Or at least he felt he did. Gravity had never felt so strong. Or so reliable. He could feel the pull of the ground and made the mistake of looking down. The ground seemed to rise up to meet him and he lost all the breath in his lungs, but a quick gulp of air, a squeeze of his eyes and a muttered prayer made his limbs move.

Lula was about twenty feet below him, a bright splash of colour against the pure white of the tower. Holding the rope in his right hand, he allowed himself to rappel steadily

down the side of the building until he came level with his
beloved Lula.

'Hi.' He tried to sound casual—as if this was something
he did every day.

Her large brown eyes looked out at him from beneath
her fringe of many colours. 'Hi.'

'You need some help?'

'Are you offering?' She gave a nervous laugh and attempted to look down.

'Don't look down! Don't look down…just…look at me.
I'm here.'

He reached out and rubbed her arm and she closed her
eyes with gratitude.

'I think I tried to do too much. I always knew heights
would be the death of me.'

He looked nervously around them. 'Well, let's hope not.
Will you listen to me? Let me help you?'

She rested her forehead against the rope. 'You want to
help me? After what I did?'

'Do we need to talk about this up here? Can this not wait
until we reach terra firma?'

'I hurt you.'

Ah, so we are talking about it up here.

'Yes, but that's okay, because since you've been gone
it's clarified everything for me.'

She glanced his way. 'You see my point of view?'

'No. Not at all. You think your only value to me is that
of procreation? What about love? What about being connected? About being soul mates?'

'You think we're soul mates?'

'Don't you?'

She grimaced. 'It's hard to think clearly up here.'

The wind blew them slightly and she gasped and gripped
the rope tighter.

'Are you kidding? This is the clearest I've ever thought!

Lula? Lula, you can do this. Listen to me. You need to feed the rope through your right hand, nice and slow. As you do that you need to walk your toes down the side of the building. Little bits… That's it. Keep doing that.'

They were moving again, but he could see she was still terrified. Her legs were trembling and kept losing contact with the tower. He kept pace with her, staying level, making reassuring comments as she kept the rope moving.

'There are thousands of successful marriages in this world, Lula, where couples don't have children. Our happiness together is not based on that being the only criteria.'

'Easy for you to say *now.*'

He could hear the shakiness in her voice. 'Easy for me to say because it's true. I *love* you, Lula! Would I have come all this way—would I be abseiling down this tower for you—if I didn't love you?'

She looked at him and met his gaze. 'No.'

'You're my everything. I've been lost without you in Atlee Wold. Everything seems darker without you there. You put *light* into my life.'

Lula stopped. 'Light?'

The ground was getting closer, but they were still very high.

He reached out and laid his hand upon hers. 'Beautiful, bright light. It doesn't matter to me if we don't have children because I'll always have *you*, and if we decide that we want to have them in some other way, then that's good, too! We could get cats or dogs—they can be our family in the meantime. And if cats and dogs are too tame for you then we'll get something crazy—like an alpaca or a snake!'

She smiled at him. 'I've always wanted a house rabbit.'

'There you go! Lula, tell me you'll come back with me. That you'll come back with me and marry me and be with me in Atlee Wold!'

Lula looked up at how far they'd come. She'd done some

of it on her own, but she'd accomplished far more with Olly at her side.

'Olly? Will you wait for me at the bottom?'

He frowned. 'What do you mean?'

'I think I can do this now. It's not far. Let me finish this abseil on my own. I'll meet you at the bottom and we'll talk then.'

'Are you sure you can do it on your own?'

'Abseiling? Yes.'

Olly nodded and rappelled down the last few feet to the bottom. She heard people clapping and cheering as she got closer and risked a glance down. It wasn't far. There were people, and boats on the water. All those faces looking up— looking at *her*. It felt right to finish the abseil on her own. It had been *her* challenge and she was determined to complete it—as she had done all the others. It was just that on some occasions, such as this, it helped to have Olly at her side.

Did she always have to do stuff alone? The way she had her entire life?

No. She didn't.

She'd found her mother at last—was there any reason she couldn't have Olly, too? Apart from the one thing she feared…?

But if she lost him because she walked away now, wouldn't that hurt just as much? She'd already faced that fear and lived through the pain of losing Olly once. But he'd offered a lifeline. A second chance. And there was no reason not to take it because if it was true what he said—that he could be happy with just her—then wouldn't they *both* be happy for many years together? Wasn't that worth more than worrying about something that might never happen?

What was that saying? *'Tis better to have loved and lost than never to have loved at all…*

Her heart soared at the possibility of hope. Hope that she could consider being with Olly and going back to Atlee

Wold and Patrick and her mother and all the other wonderful people she'd met there.

As her feet touched the ground she felt Olly's arms embrace her and he turned her round to shower her face with kisses. She could hardly breathe, but that didn't matter—because Olly was there and together they could face anything! Wrapping her arms around him, she pulled him tight before they had to separate and remove their harnesses and helmets.

The man at the bottom presented them both with a T-shirt. Written across it was *I took the scenic route*.

Lula looked at it and laughed.

She'd done it!

Sitting in a cafeteria overlooking the waterfront, Lula stirred her tea and stared at Olly. She couldn't get enough of just looking at him. At one time she'd thought that she would never see his face again, and today here he was—her knight in shining armour, who'd rescued her from a tower!

'Would you really consider having a pet snake?' she asked, smiling.

Olly reached out and took her fingers in his own. 'I would do anything for you. You know that.' He smiled, then had a thought. 'Just don't expect me to hold it.'

'I quite like boa constrictors...'

'If that's what it takes.' He squeezed her fingers and smiled.

'We could also have a dog, if you wanted something a bit more traditional. I am prepared to compromise.'

Olly lifted her fingers to his lips and kissed her. 'All great relationships are based on it.'

'Is that what you think we'll have? A great relationship?'

'I don't think it. I know it. I feel amazing when I'm with you. I feel alive—I feel the whole world has woken up and I can see everything so clearly. It's right that we're together.'

'And if I wanted to pursue…other things…would that affect us?'

'Other things? What? More crazy stunts?'

She looked at him. 'Children. Babies. I want them, Olly. I spent so many years telling myself that I didn't, but I was lying to myself. Maybe I am a traditionalist at heart? But fertility treatment can be hard. Difficult. It can break people. That's what I'm scared of. Right now I know I can't have kids, and I've accepted that, but if we go down other routes and I accept the hope that I might get pregnant somehow…but it all fails anyway…I'm not sure I could live with the disappointment.'

'Not us. I'll go through every step of it with you. With every ounce of my being. If it doesn't work out then we'll be upset and saddened, but it won't end us. We're stronger than that—we're bigger than that.'

'But how do you *know*?'

'Because we'll be in it together. Because we'll have made the choice together. I know my own heart. Even if I can't have children with you I will still have *you*. And you are so precious to me…'

'And if we can? If something can be done?'

'Then that will be amazing.' He looked deep into her eyes. 'I was so proud of you today. Conquering your fear. Finishing by yourself. Even though you scared me half to death.'

'Scared you? How?'

'By telling me you wanted to finish it alone. I thought you'd tell that to me, too.'

She shook her head. 'I couldn't.'

'No?'

'No. When I left you in the village, as I drove away, my heart broke in two. I had to stop around the corner because I couldn't drive. I couldn't see. I was crying so much and I have never experienced pain like it. You have no idea what it took me to carry on driving. To carry on putting distance between me and you. I couldn't go through that again. I wouldn't survive it.'

Olly got up from his seat opposite and slid into the chair next to her, putting his arm around her shoulders. 'I wept like a child when you left. On my knees, in the road. I didn't care who saw me. Then I had weeks of patients coming in and telling me that *they* were sad you'd left, and I wanted to rage at each and every one of them—ask them, *What about me?*'

'What did you do?'

'I hoped you'd come back. I hoped that somehow something would make you turn around and come back. And then I realised that maybe you thought you couldn't.'

'I *was* coming back.'

He smiled. 'You were?'

'I couldn't bear to be away from you.' She reached out and clasped his hand. 'My mother told you where I was, didn't she?'

He smiled. 'Accidentally. I think she was embarrassed by having me sobbing all over her kitchen floor and she did it to get rid of me,' he joked.

Lula smiled. 'I'm glad she told you. Because if she hadn't then I would have come back to you. I've given up my job at the surgery. I couldn't work, I couldn't concentrate—all I could think of was what I'd lost…'

They looked into each other's eyes and Olly leaned in to kiss her, his eyes closing softly as his lips met hers and the tender sweetness of their connection made his heart sing with joy.

When he opened his eyes again and saw her dark chocolate eyes staring into his he stroked her cheek. 'Never leave me.'

'I won't.'

'You're everything to me.'

'And you to me.'

He reached into his pocket and pulled out a small jew-
ellery box in red velvet. Opening it, he revealed a gold
ring, set with a sapphire and surrounded by diamonds that
glinted and shone in the light. 'Will you marry me, Lula?'

She looked at the ring, then at him, at the hope in his
eyes, at the love she saw burning bright from within him,
and knew that she could spend the rest of her life with this
man.

'Yes!'

Beaming with joy, he took the ring from its box and
slid it onto her finger. It was a perfect fit and he kissed her
once again. 'I found it when I was sorting out Moonrose
Cottage. It belonged to my grandmother.'

'It's beautiful.'

'Like you.'

They sank into each other's embrace and kissed again.

EPILOGUE

THE MARRIAGE OF Dr Louisa Chance to Dr Oliver James took place in the village church of Atlee Wold. Lula asked Bonnie and Ruby to be her bridesmaids, and decked them out in gorgeous red satin dresses. Ruby's daughter, Adele, toddled up the aisle, throwing rose petals everywhere.

It was a beautiful day for a summer wedding, and the whole village turned out to see it.

It had been a delight for Lula to return to Atlee. Everyone had been thrilled to see her, but none more so than her own mother.

Elizabeth Love had become a changed woman. Her poor neglected house, in which the only welcome guests had once been animals, was now often filled with villagers. She and Lula would often hold tea parties to raise funds for the animals, or for children's charities.

Everyone knew the story of Lula and Elizabeth. And no one could miss the love story between Lula and Oliver. It became the talk of the village for many years, and three years after the wedding, when Lula became pregnant, after a lot of help from medical science, the whole village waited with bated breath for the outcome!

She'd gone through so much with the IVF. She'd shared all her trials and tribulations of tests and the injecting of hormones. She'd never complained when she'd blown up like a balloon from all the medication and her ovaries had gone into overdrive and yet still only given up three eggs for harvesting.

A single egg had developed and it had looked healthy.

All their hopes and dreams focused on one tiny cell…

Lula had been her usual unconventional self and opted to go for a home birth, in a pool, listening to rock music and stroking the family dog, Buddy. When their baby daughter had been born, eleven hours after contractions had started, they'd all let out a sigh of relief.

The villagers knew the story of Lula's childhood. They knew how much being a mother meant to her. And everyone had rejoiced at the safe arrival of baby Mabel.

Tears of joy had streamed down Lula's cheeks. She'd gone from being rootless and without family to gaining a mother, a husband and now a baby daughter of her own.

She'd got roots. She'd got family. The two things she'd thought impossible and yet had craved her whole life.

And, to celebrate, she added the colour green to her hair.

* * * * *

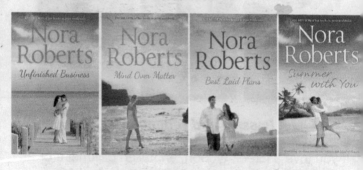

MILLS & BOON®

MEDICAL ROMANCE™

THE ULTIMATE IN ROMANTIC MEDICAL DRAMA

A sneak peek at next month's titles...

In stores from 1st May 2015:

- **Always the Midwife** – Alison Roberts *and*
  Midwife's Baby Bump – Susanne Hampton

- **A Kiss to Melt Her Heart** – Emily Forbes *and*
  Tempted by Her Italian Surgeon – Louisa George

- **Daring to Date Her Ex** – Annie Claydon

- **The One Man to Heal Her** – Meredith Webber
